The Late Japanese
and other stories

D E Young

to Judit and John,

with love,

Doreen

15th May 2017

Published 2017 by arima publishing
www.arimapublishing.com

ISBN 978 1 84549 706 4
© D E Young 2017

Printed and bound in the United Kingdom
Typeset in Garamond

In this work of fiction, the characters, places and events are
either the product of the author's imagination or they are used
entirely fictitiously. Any resemblance to actual persons, living
or dead, is purely coincidental.

arima publishing
ASK House, Northgate Avenue
Bury St Edmunds, Suffolk IP32 6BB
t: (+44) 01284 700321
www.arimapublishing.com

for

Alan, my husband,
and Naomi and Gareth,
Francis and Rachel, the family.

Preface

This second volume of my Short Stories will prove how I relish the opportunity the Short Story gives to unpick and re-form a narrative whether known, remembered or imagined.

In this volume my stories cover a varied range of human experience. In them I have aimed to be incisive, taut and expressive in style, whilst opening up vistas and landscapes which my readers can inhabit for themselves. There are themes of family, discovery, threat and joyous eccentricity threading through each story, be it light or dark.

There can be no story without a setting, nor yet that of its writer. I have mine in and around St. Edmundsbury Cathedral where the Cathedral Library staff give me both space and personal tonic in an ideal setting. Margaret, Ricky, Paul, Penelope and Alan help me to flourish. Staff at the Pilgrims' Kitchen daily provide a welcome atmosphere where I can comfortably be left alone to write.

My publisher, Richard, is to be thanked warmly for his generous help alongside the busy life of his publishing world. My best friends, Karen and Margaret and my sister, Joan, who have read each story with an attentive and critical eye deserve a special mention and Judy, my proofreader, too, who has come up for air each time with a smile. Such is the nature of the short story, absorbing, memorable and there to enjoy.

D.E. Young, April 2017

Contents

The Candle and the Cross

It would be unwise for Joyce to point out everything in the small front room of her home. It was so filled with her painting and sewing that one theatrical wave towards the fireplace was enough to indicate every burst of colour which filled her life.

Teaching art and textiles can't possibly be easy, thought her guests, sympathetic to the riot and blaze in this room, but when Joyce began to speak, then they pitied her students.

This was a woman of stridency. Her vowels were created in long and short stitch, the consonants couched and thickly overlain and her flow of words punctuated by that very exact pause when the needle enters coarse material or the brush is poised about an escaping landscape. So few could like Joyce Wildsmith. Her older exam students teased, 'Mith Wildsmith', so that the younger pupils would poke fun in return.

'Look at that outfit today. How could she make it, let alone wear it?'

'She's not one in a million. She's a complete solo act.'

Joyce resembled a Pierrot figure in wide dirndl skirts, outfits which she had made herself using paper patterns of the Fifties. There was always a colour clash somewhere on the outfit. The clown's vibrant diamonds lived on in her rings and bracelets, in mismatched scarves and coloured leather shoes. Joyce very rarely gave the impression of choosing what to wear, rather a whole colour palette spilled itself haphazardly. The carefree abandon with which she flaunted this complete lack of dress sense on a figure which grew in girth as she aged, further accentuated the theatrical and its very poorly-written play at that. Most wished that the curtain would soon come down.

Could an age be put on this person of presence? Probably not. Joyce looked as if mid-life crisis had been her lot since adolescence and what few wrinkles she had accumulated were not on account of age but of the close work of embroidery and appliqué which occupied her evenings. Her body movements were quick and unusual, so that determining age was not easy. She rarely kept still. It was as if she was always about to go on

5

stage to a play in which she had a much smaller part than anticipated. She came into every room with a large bag, determined to bounce, not to make an entrance but to catch at herself as she tripped forward, the flounce of her skirts aiming for the floor like a back row ballerina. Catching up with herself in this manner was followed by the huff and puff to recover, so that preliminary conversation could only concern her and her needs.

'Have you got what you want, Joyce?'

Perhaps an unfinished tapestry trailed from her bag like a peahen's feather, a doleful comment on an incessant needle, another project to be tacked into place unredeemed.

'I'll get it all together in a minute. 5A should be slaughtered. They're a month off exams for God's sake!'

'I think we're all finding them a pain.'

'Have you got a minute, Trevor?' Joyce called.

'No, not exactly, Joyce. I might see you at lunch.'

Who could speak meaningfully to this peacock of circumstance, blazing a formidable colour scheme to the opposite sex and so concerned to be adorable in the ugliness of her choice of clothes and self-willed conversation? The small head atop the flamboyance moved from side to side even as she spoke, concerned to spot anyone within earshot whom she could engage in a current tirade.

Yet, sheer brilliance of skill and supreme intelligence shone through, no-one would deny, as they fled to all corners of a room which Joyce entered, fearful, excusing, flurried, in case conversation caused them to be rude to this poor woman.

She was not that. You could tell from the fabrics she chose that more than common sense ruled her every choice. Hers was the dedication to an ideal despite the lack of the ideal figure, the steady deportment, the small feet, the balanced personality. Joyce was made to flow, even if it was over rocky surfaces, on areas which snagged and lives which turned upon her and teased. She chose colours and clothing of determination because that was her real character, not the comic which others found it so easy to see.

'Joyce, what kind of outfit is that?' her perplexed parents must have reasoned, and in days when fabric was hard to get, she had saved for tulle and poplin and flounced off to Art School as their headstrong, only child.

Then came a week in the middle of the school term when a couple of phone calls led to a commission from a Cathedral in the Home Counties. A gentleman's voice spoke.

'Keep to the theme of the Roman interpretation of the site. Get the airy feel of the grounds we are set in. When can you get down to see us?'

Joyce chose a date in a breezy April, just before Easter. She drove down in her ageing Triumph and met the Dean over an afternoon tea.

Dr. Donwell was attempting to reach back beyond his time at the Cathedral.

'We're anxious, Miss Wildsmith, to serve the town and county with which your family have had such a firm connection. Your father's time here has not been forgotten. He made so much of ecumenical links in the Methodist tradition. I'm told he was truly one of us, too.'

These dapper comments meant very little to Joyce, although the Dean didn't see her eyes glaze over as he observed their bright restlessness. With her duck-diving movements of head and shoulders, she seemed to need to shrug off any conversation like water.

'I'm working on a mixed media piece. The cross will glow above a candle set to one side, all on navy blue or perhaps deep teal.'

'Just the one candle, Miss Wildsmith? They are two stark symbols.'

'They might very well be, but it's their juxtaposition which counts.' Joyce bent over to roughly sketch a plain, blocked cross on the top left and a candle, thick and as chunky as the cross, bottom right.'

'Yes, I see, but is there a juxtaposition if the two symbols are the same size?'

'It will all depend on the background colour, as I see it. I'll balance both if the two symbols are shown held in the darkness together. Can you show me where the commission will be hung?'

Later that afternoon, the two made their way to the West door. Joyce was walking jerkily beside a distinguished man who became used to her knocking him with an elbow or an arm as they walked.

'The Ecumenical Chapel is to be incorporated into the crypt. We reach it this way.'

The stairs were not a hazard until Joyce came to the top step. The swaying skirts warned her companion in advance.

'I'll go ahead, if you'll forgive me.'

'Not at all,' came the reply from one who might have abseiled down, given an opportunity.

In the underground space, Joyce shed her flamboyance as if she had undressed for bed. A certainty of quiet behaviour gave her companion confidence.

'Miss Wildsmith, the space where your commission will hang is a little gloomy at the moment, but we intend to bring in lighting which will complement what you produce. Here we are.'

The corner area Dr. Donwell showed her was boxed between a small altar and a smaller cupboard, such that an icon might serve the space best. Joyce was convinced about the dark blue of her surround and she set out to reassure the gentleman beside her.

'This space is ideal. It will become enlarged with the clarity of the symbols, but it won't take away from the prominence of the altar.'

'That remains plain.' Dr. Donwell spoke with some relief.

Joyce turned in the narrow space to look carefully up at the man who had made the phone calls. A quietly reassuring look came from the well-set head held on the narrow shoulders of a tall frame. Joyce hadn't noted this whilst sat in his office earlier. In this quirk of circumstance, she was all out to serve her commission, not herself. She was well away from home and school and she felt freed. This man who had to listen to her was easily able to make her listen to him.

'When we get back, would you be able to stay a little longer? I've got biscuits and cheese over at the Deanery.'

The two strolled together across a strip of grass. Seen from a distance, a tall stick of a man appeared to be trailing a large, open, lady's umbrella.

Motoring back, Joyce was at the wheel with the images of candle and cross on each side of her forward gaze, especially on the motorway, when she stayed in the centre lane.

'What do you mean, Miss Wildsmith? How do you make a centre of dark?' This able student attempting to understand her tutor was a rarity. Melissa was hoping for an explanation.

Joyce began to sketch the corner for her. 'Altar there, my work hanging higher and the cross should be on the altar. It's not. It's on the right wall.' She drew sight lines across to the wall.

'When I centre up the darkness, the gold cross and white candle will cross over, touch, you know, in the mind's eye, and sit right on top of one another, doubly bright.'

A long necklace she was wearing that day jangled on the table as she was sketching her idea.

'I've been invited back. I've just got to get on with it now.'

Every embroiderer would know how ugly the first stitches of stump work look when laid down. The laced-over padding of a leaf to be embroidered might resemble a cold sliced potato on the background silk. Figures as forthright as Joyce's, the upright and the cross with right angles looked like safari tyre treads over precious blue glass. But this was a woman with fistfuls of energy. Sleeves rolled up out of the way of snagging the work in hand, Joyce stitched the off-white thread for the candle on top of silver not just for bulk, but to catch light in any of the minute areas where her stitching might expand.

'I'll bring in a piece of my plan for the cross. It's never going to come your way as a subject, you'll be glad to know.'

Melissa smiled at that.

'It will be in a chevron stitch, gold thread under. I probably won't be able to spare any for a sample when it comes to it.'

As a geometric exercise, the cross had to be treated with caution. Joyce sewed the sloped padding of the four arms as if it was uphill work for all of its two foot height. The crossover with its four triangular humps had padding pushed down with a crochet hook and smoothed with the pressing of a palette knife. Alone at home, Joyce's fidgeting figure prodded and tamed the single cross, humming to herself, denied any of the conversation that Ecclesiastical embroiderers in their sewing groups might enjoy. She came to rely on some frequent phone calls.

'I can't quite take it in,' Melissa said as she attempted to identify with all the hard work and effort in front of her. Miss Wildsmith had brought in the unframed silk on a Monday morning. The lethargy of that time of day left Melissa at a stroke. Very boldly, to the upper left side of an intensely dark blue, sat a cross condensed into air. The outline, in a minute feather stitching, enabled the creation to escape from its density of background and project an inner dynamic. Ridged cream and gold stitching sat comfortably close as soon as the eye considered it, looking fresh, not overworked.

'I really like it, Miss Wildsmith. I never thought I would, you know. Can I touch it?' She put a finger on the upraised work coving gently up from the silk.

Alongside, the candle looked incongruously out of context, as a light in its own right, but Joyce was adamant still about the geometric need for it to be there.

'Trouble is, Melissa, we'll never know once it's framed. I couldn't make any photograph do it justice in the crypt. It's very unlikely many will see it, but you and I will know it's there. Get on with your work. You've got an exam to pass. I want you to pass creditably because I won't be teaching you next term. I want your new tutor to be quite sure how good you are.'

'Miss Wildsmith, where are you going?'

'I'm going to be married. We have a house in the Cathedral grounds.'

The Late Japanese

Cécile's placement at a language School in Chartres was a bonus of a job. The Cathedral towered over her thoughts as it did to Woodhouse & Welby's's fifty pupil School in a four-storeyed town house, refurbished for numerous uses. It lent itself to the style of school not common in France, but was usual in most Cathedral cities of England from which Cécile had come. She had come to Europe for a post so English in style, it could take on Chartres itself. Twenty five girls needed to be taught and kept safe until they returned to Russia or the Far East in a month's time. Only then would Cécile have her own holiday break.

'Can't they get by?' Cécile called to a taxi driver filling the hallway of the house. Two girls from Taiwan had gone ahead of him and were looking confused at the bottom of the stairs. Some of these girls had been to a number of Language Schools and knew the impetus of moving onwards into any type of accommodation. Others, reticent after a long journey, hovered at the foot of stairs as if life was enacted on one floor only.

'Well, I've got them to you. They're yours now.' The driver turned to her as he spoke. 'Bertrand will be next here. There's been a bit of a delay at Orly.'

It was a Sunday and a very busy day at the Cathedral close by. Cécile worked over the sound of bells and the scrape of feet as tourists passed her ground floor window. She had a flat with a bedroom and a sitting room office where she now sat, dealing with the paperwork. She had done the same a fortnight ago, when the course began. Girls and boys had arrived and were allocated their rooms. Taxi drivers had been tipped, the girls had measured up Mrs. Goodwin and mostly reacted well. Like the Maître in the Catholic schools of France, of which the girls knew nothing, Cécile and her staff turned down beds, checked on friendships and provided any forgotten basics, then left everyone to themselves. It was at this two week point that there was a turnover of ten or so teenagers. Now was the delivery of the very last of her charges.

'It's a Japanese girl I'm waiting for. She's from Osaka.'

'He'll let you know when her plane lands, then it's forty minutes, knowing Bertrand.'

Two hundred metres up the narrow road was the School house fitted out for teaching and dining. Such places were once the focus of French towns. The gaunt wall with wooden double doors opened on a courtyard and for them this evening, to a meal at six o'clock before the place was locked for the night.

Cécile's younger co-helper, Louise, was upstairs to explain the final plans for the day then rang the hall bell to summon the queue for the count of heads before the five minute walk up to the evening meal.

No phone call had been received nor a text, so Cécile decided to go up with all the girls and get to know the new ones. The boys, housed in the adjacent building, were always so much taller than the girls. They were likely to be progressing to Business Schools after a well-funded education.

Cécile and Jacques sat to compare notes.

'I'm done for the day, Cecile. Have you got all your girls?' Jacques sat down quite heavily.

'One to go. This could be her,' said Cécile as her mobile buzzed. 'Yes, and I'll have to go back, Jacques. I can't have her waiting outside the locked building. I'll be less than ten minutes.'

Cécile left her charges to their meal and crossed the courtyard to the large gates. The cobbled street was still hazed with hot sunshine from the afternoon. It would be difficult to run, but the narrow pavement allowed Cécile a quick one up, one down movement of leg and thigh, which got her along perfectly well.

All the while Cécile wondered about the late Japanese. She knew her name, of course, Tomeo, who wanted to be known as Tomi. Her best language was English and her parents were in London until she returned.

Cécile rounded the corner to look up the street, along to the Cathedral's south doors. The lowering sun gleamed its thousand years of heat upon the statues, setting shadows stark and playing on pitted faces for the few seconds Cécile paid them attention. Leaning on the car door of a blue taxi cab and holding a pink attaché case was a slight girl. The driver stood with one large suitcase at the Language School door. Cecile was composed as she walked up, waving a hand in acknowledgement to them both.

'Tomeo? I'm Madame Goodwin. Welcome to Chartres and our Language School.'

Tomeo gave Cécile a smile distinctively polite and stepped forward with her to open the door and carry in her cases. The taxi driver called an 'A bientôt' to Tomeo as he drove away.

Cécile's last piece in the puzzle for the final fortnight of the course, was walking beside her on the cobbles. Cécile towered over her on the narrow pavement.

It was difficult to tell if Tomeo looked puzzled from the angle at which Cécile walked with her. It was clear, that just like the others, she would prefer her own age group. That was nicely normal and a thought to keep Cécile on track as she took Tomeo along to her late supper with the others.

'Let's get them up to bed,' Cécile murmured to Louise a great deal later that evening. The lengthening afternoon had walked into its own sleep. Not so these teenagers teetering on the edge of strangeness, staying away from sleep as long as they dared.

Cécile was used to the noise above her, a bevy of all their lives, unknown, including the late Japanese. That final jigsaw piece, as Cécile could see from looking into her dormitory door, was placed just right in the scheme of things.

'Can't say I'll be up much longer, Cécile,' yawned Louise when she came back to her. It was 10pm. 'They won't like lessons tomorrow, though. There's too much social buzz.'

'They'll settle down. It's this halfway point, supposedly to shake up the mix. After registration, I'm meeting Jacques in the city - Mirmo's. We'll both have a breathing space after the rush.'

Cécile tried to sound relieved about the new relaxation, but it did not come easily. Last evening had been a heavy one for late July. The surrounding fields rapidly dried the air which came in from the local streams to circulate the Cathedral. It could be seen many kilometres away, comforted from below its cantilevered waist, like incense warming upward from thuribles old as time. The dimming light silenced the local streets. Beyond Chartres, villages clattered. The population would be largely away for August.

'I'll be gone by early August. Two more weeks. Too much time to think of two long weeks.' Cécile's fitful sleep was accorded an early morning's worth of rational endeavour.

'Good morning, girls. Get yourselves up and about. We leave for breakfast at the third bell.'

Louise prompted Cécile's plans for the day.

'Unless I hear otherwise, I've got the girls all afternoon for tennis.'

'Were the new girls all right, as far as you know?'

'Oh, yes. You'll see at registration.'

Walking up to the School that morning, twenty teenage girls straddled the cool pavement shadow. Some called out in Russian to catch up. Tomeo was with the two Taiwanese, diminutive together, but not short on dress sense.

Lessons began in classrooms around the School compound. Only the sound of a trolley being taken into position over the courtyard gravel for the morning coffee broke the silence as Cécile left for the centre of Chartres. She closed the courtyard door, confident in her half morning bonus after the busy weekend. She could take a quicker walk than her meandering girls. She would soon turn to find the Cathedral ahead.

She did none of these things but stopped and leaned against the wall bent over at the waist at a quite awful and sudden pain. She looked up to calculate the distance to her front room Office, her bed, her chair. She could not move her legs forward without pain so frightening it took her breath away. It was at the very top of both legs, racking those muscles with spasms which she had no way of calculating or controlling. Cécile held on to the wall with both hands attempting breaths of the sort which might help.

'I shouldn't have gone back for Tomeo in such a hurry. I've pulled muscles at the top of my legs.' Cécile's thoughts were being debarred even as they quickened to cope with a pain so severe. She texted Jacques:- 'Find me at flat, 0900'. Then came the walking. No-one was in this side road so early and it stretched ahead and round its corner like a lunar landscape, strange to footprints or a lurching woman, bravely stepping onwards and along as if on clumsy skis.

Very slowly, Cécile tried lifting her right leg to massage it at the top. Nothing changed. The presence of severe pain produces no variation. Cécile moved the leg forward and cried out in terror. She did not move it. Instead, she shuffled sideways along the cool wall opposite the school, where a courtyard beyond would hold no persons to hear her call. Sound, silence, concentration and the piercing sense of needing to control such an unknown, enveloped her all together. Sound she cut out. Silence aided her measured steps and focus. Her plight continued as she balanced and swung her legs along. Her pelvis screamingly ached at every step and at every three or four moves Cécile stopped to breathe more easily.

She managed, just somehow, to arrive at the corner. She rounded it, gripping the wall, as tree-huggers do breathing into soft bark. She heard Jacques call.

'Cécile! What on earth?' He rushed up and instinctively held on to her shoulders.

'I just don't know what has happened. My top legs are in such pain I can hardly move except below the knee.'

'Let's get you to lie down, and painkillers as quick as possible.'

Thank heaven Jacques was in managing mode. Cécile knew rare relief as she heard the key in the door of the house. There would be a bed to lie on, to stop the movement which produced this dizzying and inexplicable pain.

'I can't believe this is happening, Jacques. You saw me at breakfast. I was okay then.'

Lying down on her bed in that downstairs room, Cécile was relieved of almost half of the pain. It dimmed as it throbbed at her new prone position.

'I hope these painkillers will do the trick.' Jacques had opened the small medicine cupboard on the wall near her bed.

'If you'll get me some water, please. I'll take two each of these. The cleaner will be here in half an hour. She's pretty good at things, but I'll perk up soon.'

In the ten minutes before Madame Bonnay arrived, Cécile huddled down in the bedclothes to keep warm. Her shivering body was rattling the areas of pain at the top of her legs. Flat on her back was best and she couldn't continue her teaching job in that position. Cécile hurried through the possibilities brought about only twenty minutes before and less than a couple of hundred metres away.

Madame Bonnay slammed the front door behind her and peered into Cécile's room.

'Madame! Are you ill?'

Cécile explained very briefly. Madame Bonnay went to fill a hot water bottle for the shivering Cécile and came back full of concern.

'It's so sudden, so sudden,' she scolded, meaning that she needed to get on with her work. Eventually, as the sounds of the house began around her, Cécile dozed. The hoover hummed its insistence that someone was using it up and down the hall, up and down the stairs, to mock the woman in bed on the ground floor.

So the sounds merged at last, none of them comforting. Cécile measured her breathing to the nuisance of pain. The droning hoover only accentuated her worry about the job she was doing that mere half hour ago.

Later that day, Cécile lay back in an Emergency unit of the Hospital a little out of the centre of Chartres. Bright lights were above her. She was lying exactly as she had been moved from her bed to this bed. She knew she had been speaking to a surgeon and she must have told him that she had walked quickly to collect the late Japanese. The man was smiling down at her and speaking kindly.

'You can be grateful to that young lady. You set all this in motion by running like you did. An abscess can lie very deep and give no warning of such serious infection. We wouldn't have been able to save you.'

The Teapot

Tim was uncannily easy to miss in a crowd. It wasn't that he was short. A firm-looking five feet ten inches defined him as average, easy to spot and even stand out, but he didn't. If it was a diffident demeanour, that wasn't it either, on first glance. He'd had an army life until redundancy at Waterbeach Barracks. You stood out there or you were kicked down the cracks they found for you.

Redundancy didn't suit him. Was that the reason for the invisibility Tim knew he had developed? He used it in as organised a manner as he could. He even phoned his wife about it.

'No, you do it, Tim. Get in an Indian on your way back.'

It must have been that particular takeaway that proved it. Are all takeaway meals about more than empty stomachs - emptied lives? Jill wasn't there when he got back as delivery boy with the two white carrier bags. No logo on them, no message in the house. She had gone. One look at the bedroom proved it.

He had folded up those two white bags quite carefully that day, put them away, relished the experience. They would come out again filled with some of the junk of her life. His would be the flat, folded, concertinaed life of the newly-single man now back to the shape he was before. He had squashed up in the Army, on parade, moving into line. Single would be fine.

The jobs didn't come along in ones, though. Contacts decreased as the time wore on. So, it was nights, shelf-filling, to keep the flow in his own life. Tim's name didn't tinkle any more. There was just the thud of tin-filled boxes on the Supermarket floor, his arms robotically taking him around jammed aisles, breathing in, detecting the invisible obstacle behind the stack, the one that tripped you up, the instance that would call up a shout at the Barracks. 'Stand out, Manson!'

Now Millie could do that. You would see her around because she was a lady too close to six feet tall to be missed. Although she had no girth of waist to negotiate, there was a manner in her long arms and jutting elbows which brought a degree of attention and notice. It was as well to adjust a close encounter accordingly.

'Oscar, move over. I've got the story book,' and long arms stretched right round the four year-old, the coloured book and the cup of coffee, if Richard brought her one.

'Super, super,' Oscar had got into saying.

It was quite a feat. Millie was of an age to be ready for working at grandchildren. Everyone had told her, 'Make some time for yourself,' but she was entwined with this new, upcoming generation in a way she had not thought she could develop.

Richard teased.

'You're in your old mode and no mistake,' as if reminding her that he hadn't taken turns on any sofa with his two daughters, at least not one he could remember over thirty years. What counted for Millie was that she was contributing to Helene, the daughter who lived the closer to them of the two, giving her some of her time, giving it her best shot.

She was due to meet up with her this coming Friday. It would be a very good thing to give Helene a break from the boy before the weekend was full on, the husband home from London after a long week and the dullness of the weather meaning a bellyful of indoors. Millie knew that feeling over and over. How full a room became when one child made it feel a gambolling herd was in its space.

Tim's time tocked away night by night.

He worked with those people of the dark coming into an invisible world, conjured, some of them, from obscure corners of Europe and placed in a colourful pack of cards as he was. He came out at night to play.

Tim found that he could work his magic on all those in-between and behind spaces on the shelves, where the customer doesn't see the odd upside down box or the split plastic packet. As he took over spaces like this, waiting to be cleared if they were noticed at all, he removed commodities to find them. He reached over packets and jars into remaindered space and gave it a reason for being there. He felt his own continuity with it and his endurance. He was learning a few more tricks.

He found that strange definiteness of the early morning hours quite cheering, so he didn't drive unhappily home for seven o'clock. A cleaned-up day lay ahead once he laid his head on a pillow. Noon rises might be rare enough. Tim made it his routine as if he had snapped to in Barracks ready for an afternoon shift.

Millie wondered where the time had gone that morning. It was fatal to look at emails and even think of phoning and it was eleven thirty before she had even thought of, then reconsidered, a biscuit.

'I can't get ahead, Richard,' she called out to him at one point. 'I'm still treading water.'

'That's life now, Millie,' Richard almost shouted back. 'Hadn't you noticed?'

She had. It was Millie, the urgently needed, Millie, the much anticipated, Millie, the indispensable, of many things than the time before Oscar.

Richard had come into the room.

'Who really rules the world now?' she said to him, clicking her laptop shut. 'It's little Oscars. The under-fives are like a brain drain on us, don't you think? I'm a passenger service, bespoke child-minder, cook and downtime manufacturer!'

Richard smiled.

'Do I sound like an American advert? I don't mean it, but you know what I think about time to ourselves. Where did it all go?'

'Or do you mean, 'where does it all go?' There's a difference.'

'Not so I'd notice. What would you like for lunch before I get off to Helene?'

Tim's lunch came to hand quite gracefully. One of his tricks was mastered at a well-known Coffee Chain. Snacks, lunch sandwiches and salads were in the cabinet at the front door. Tim worked out the times of the lunchtime handover of staff during a couple of visits for coffee. When they were head down, or their backs were turned, he took the edibles, usually a sandwich pack, to the rear of the queue and then slipped onto a nearby table with his stolen lunch. There might be an uncollected mug or two to broadly convince that he had been there at a quick glance. Any grabbed sandwich tasted heavenly. They were always sweet, when the stale air of the night job hadn't quite left him after the morning sleep. Often egg mayonnaise or tuna clung freshly to the cellophane slope of the packaging, giving him a sense of being well-filled, along with the sandwich.

Lunch behind him, Tim also had an occasional take on afternoon tea. He helped himself to teabags from the rest room tub, a couple at a time, and when the opportunity arose, sat some afternoons in a small restaurant where hot water comes in a separate pot to the tea. Nicely brewing his own at table, he might only need to ask for the extra milk which they were bound to provide a discerning customer. Anything free suited this night bee whose pollen sacs were never full enough, filling shelves for those who had more to spend in a week than he in a month of Sundays.

Millie and Helene had a midpoint meeting, where two cars could be parked without problem, and none better a venue than a Supermarket Car Park. The small cafeteria just inside the wide front doors spread its few tables along the front windows, one of which had a notice to explain that a free tea or coffee could be yours with a counter purchase. Millie liked the promise before or after her shopping and so did a great many shoppers, and if you chose your time for a beverage, it could be a comforting half hour without any sense of favour or gain, just goodwill all round.

'Round about quarter to three, then, Helene?'

'That'll suit nicely Mum, just before schools are out. I'm picking up Oscar from Nursery at half past four, then it's over to you, as you know.'

'I'll be there, Helene.'

Nothing more than a rendezvous very little out of the ordinary would take up almost the whole afternoon by the time she arrived. Millie chose to change into a long grey skirt, loose enough to be around Oscar, smart enough for a café close to town and often frequented by her friends when they shopped.

'Nice jacket, Mum. Is that recent?'

'No Helene. I got it last year.' Millie spoke as they were both lining up at the Cafeteria counter. Hot food from the lunch time still steamed and bubbled on a hot plate as they pushed their tray by.

'I'm just having a pot of tea, Helene. I can steal a few treats to eat when I have Oscar.'

'I'll have a cup of coffee. I won't go for a big mug.'

They took their tray to a table for two along the far side wall and sat to chat about Helene's busy morning and the break she needed that evening.

'I'm happy to do it. You know I am, Helene.'

Tim barely heard the two in conversation alongside his table. He had been there for a while with his pot of tea and hot water. He had his back to them both but had seen them lining up. What mother and daughter didn't catch up on conditions of life? From a vantage point of hardly conceivable comfort they conceived of more, cushioning their lives all the time with the next plan and the next commitment, and there'd be a man somewhere having to listen to it all again this evening. Tim had done with that. He had said a firm farewell to wagging tongues some time ago. He lived between walls which didn't really know him as he hardly ever spoke, but listened. He could still appreciate variety of tone and spot occasional circumstance.

One presented itself now. After a shorter time than anticipated, the two ladies on the table behind him got up to leave. They passed his table still in the middle of a conversation and made their way to the exit.

Tim's right arm reached out behind him and his face turned just enough to see the teapot which had been left by the two women. With a dexterity not often seen in the area of cafeteria tables, Tim picked up the teapot, slowly turned with it and poured himself the remaining cup of his neighbours' tea. He did not need to return the pot. He simply sat to drink from his refilled cup.

In his job, Tim stood to fill shelves on empty Supermarket floors. In this restaurant who knows where feet will take you? The two ladies got up to choose a cake each at the counter and stood, obviously intending to return to their place. Who placed them there to do that? Tim spotted just enough wriggle room and no more. He slipped soundlessly from his table onto theirs, from his warmed seat to Helene's vacated one. It was a starker view from there, a less comforting circumstance than envisaged and, as the two ladies became aware that someone had taken their space, they stood together in that small cafeteria looking for a twosome table. The only one available was the one seating four vacated by Tim. Helene sat down where Tim had been, oblivious of any sleight of hand or deviousness in so respected a place, and concentrated on her slice of cake. Millie sat to face the Supermarket door. She was smoothing her skirt when she saw over Helene's shoulder a friend of her husband's.

'There's Roger. I wonder if he'd like a cup of tea with us?'

Alice's Farm

It didn't seem like early morning as she had been certain it was, and the dirt path which should have been soundless under her slippers was gravel, scrunching underfoot. Her usual path was blocked by a tractor placed across it like a barrier. She knew what was on the other side, even though it was clear she was not supposed to move on round it.

It was her farm, their farm, a family farm in mid-Norfolk, built by the river which defined the area of the Wensum. Set low down in the valley floor only fifty metres or so from the river bank, the farmhouse behind her was sturdily built against the river's draughts and chill. Alice looked back at the porch. It was crenellated in brick to a centre point just like a Church porch. Inside was a safe house, the home she had made for the boys. Church porches would have had marriages performed in them, but farmhouse porches were for Harvest revellers, men sat together with those long pipes. She had used it for boots and umbrellas for much of her time as keeper of the house.

'Alf? You about?' Her call was subdued as if she'd find him in the porch she had just left.

'Alice, isn't it?' came a soft voice instead, and a woman dressed in a black tee shirt and trousers came round the parked tractor as if she had been cued to do so.

She had.

'Who are you? I don't know you,' said Alice to the face in front of her with its dyed, bobbed fair hair framing an urgent look. She saw the headphones around the woman's neck.

'You do, Alice. I'm Gemma. Can I get you a cup of tea upstairs?'

Upstairs, in a bed-sitting room, where Gemma led Alice that morning, she explained again that there were visitors to her farm for the next three weeks and that Alice would see a great many people about if she looked from her window. Hadn't she remembered that she wasn't to come down? Her son, Bob, was coming every day to get her meals so that the visitors could get on with improving the farmyard and putting the place to rights.

'You know we've done a lot in the house, Alice. You've got new lights for your staircase and the TV is the best one Bob could find for you.'

'Oh, Bob looks after me all right,' said Alice as she settled down in an armchair.

Gemma left her and glided down the back staircase and along to the farther side of the house where the morning film crew was preparing.

'I've got Alice upstairs now, so outside's clear.'

It needed to be clear for a morning inspection of the twelve evacuees chosen for the filming. They had settled to their pre-war beds and bedding the evening before, bickering amongst themselves because of strangeness and tiredness and the brightness of the lights during the short space of filming and their final lights out. They swore at the beds when the camera wasn't on them.

Alice heard none of this. It went on above her on a different floor in a far wing, where she would have put empty suitcases, boxes and cast-off clothing from the Fifties and Sixties. One girl's voice shrieked out, 'I can't sleep in this,' and perhaps Alice heard it as a mother might hear a baby's snuffle in sleep, telling her that she can turn over and begin a sounder pattern herself. Alice had turned, thinking of pyjama legs and how they caught curling toes as they were pulled on. They would be warm, though, and the snuggle down was real.

That same girl led the way out of the farmhouse door this morning. Inside, the Farmer's wife of the TV series had checked hair and nails after breakfast and had lined them up, boys in one line, girls in another and the girls came out first.

Gemma checked that both crews were filming from each side of the shambling line, catching the children's faces, mortified, excited, prepared to challenge everything from a far distant age. Each boy and girl was dressed in a type of school uniform with shorts and shirts for the boys. The girls had navy gymslips, well-creased and hanging shapelessly, to their very obvious discomfort, along with white ankle socks and brown sandals. The first school lesson in a farm barn and meeting their teacher was going to be a crucial bit of filming. A third camera crew was already in the cold barn around the side of the farmhouse. Alice looked out of her window as the twelve walked gingerly on unfamiliar gravel to a lesson destined to be a tough-going couple of hours out of sight of all movement in the yard.

The top of twelve heads of hair were beneath her small window on the second floor. Short bobs for the boys and pigtails for the girls were immediately obvious and she thought of the village children who came for apples in the orchard or who wandered up to the house for Hallowe'en and who sang at Christmas. Children ordered routine itself, but these heads were bobbing a lot and their shoulders weren't straight. What were their mothers doing to let them come? Bob must have a big job for the twelve to do and they would need biscuits at the end of it all, whatever it was. She got up to go downstairs. All the wellington boots were in the big porch.

'I'll get them sorted out.'

When children need something you can provide, a remarkable versatility of the organised mind comes into play. Alice came down the back stairs with a firm tread of ideas. She'd have a set of different sizes of boot, easily, and there were plenty of socks in one of Bob's bedroom drawers.

No-one was about as Alice neared the porch at the front. She passed her very large Drawing room which looked west over a tangled lawn and rose garden to a low-lying field, village housing and the river alongside, so close and very wide. Summer sandwiches of paste and cucumber scented her search for muddy boots, creating a dislocation between floral dresses and boots, the real distinction of a farmer's wife.

Gemma came out when she heard footsteps ahead of her in the house.

'Alice?' she gently called and moved forward in quite different mode to her producer routine.

'Alice, have you come down?' She called again and turned into the Drawing room to see her standing by the French windows, holding a pair of wellington boots.

'I've just got the one pair left for the boys and girls,' she said. 'I'll let you have them gladly. Have they all come for the farm work?'

'Yes, they have, Alice. They're all here to help you, but you can't help them very much now you've got older. I'll take them and then we can go upstairs again.'

The following day, when filming began very early on the farm, Alice wasn't up and about until almost morning coffee time. She came down the back stairs to the silence of the ground floor with thoughts of good children, well-washed hallway tiles, and a banging bucket noise in her ears from somewhere in the farm, she thought. The noise continued and grew as she walked carefully through it. It was an air raid siren, on her farm, loud and clear, and its powerful thudding was amplified by voices, children's voices.

'It's down here. We know the way.'

'Oh, help. I really don't like this.'

'Get off my back, there's stairs.'

Alice stood at the end of the corridor which ran through the house, watching boys and girls turn down to the understairs cellar doorway and disappear, talking loudly, but not laughing. Abruptly, the siren ceased and a black figure of a man with a large camera on his shoulder came along immediately. He went through the same door to descend those stone stairs.

'Here you!' she called.

The man glanced back from the third or fourth step down. Shortened by the perspective and the drop, Alice didn't find him fearful as she continued speaking.

'I've got supplies in down there, y'know. Give the children a biscuit each.'

'Yes, I will, dear,' came the reply as he continued on his way to the filming sequence.

Alice went to find a chair by the stout table in her downstairs workroom. She would get underneath it if the air raid siren turned out to be more than just a practice.

Gemma found her in that chair when she came up from the cellar.

'How do you like it down there?' said Alice with a sharp look upwards. 'This house is built very well, you know.'

'It certainly is,' said Gemma. 'The fuss is over now, so I'll take you upstairs for your better view. You don't want to be stuck down here.'

Alice went happily enough. A cup-of-tea feeling comes on with a worry over, and she put the kettle on as soon as she got upstairs. From her high-up window, the river willows were about to create their spring green waving wall alongside the Wensum. Her home was unusually close to the river's flood plain, but the farmhouse had a raised garden at the crucial distance, evidently secure, as had been proved over the years.

The days of rustlings within her farmhouse went on, but Alice was finding the sounds anything but unusual. She was not one to be told that filming was becoming surprisingly successful, despite the chill of this early Spring and Easter, nor was she told that the Bank Holiday Monday was planned to be a Church Fête on her front lawn with re-enactors of the time coming on site by bike or on foot for authenticity.

Easter Sunday was very quiet. The Church bells rang out from across the river and twelve evacuees, crews and worshippers were all at another village Church for the filming, out of the sight and mind of Alice. Her son, Bob, took her out to Sunday lunch at the village pub.

'You've been very settled in the house, Mum?' was his half query, half hopeful remark to her.

'There's been a bit of company about, but I've taken not too much notice. That's all right, isn't it, Bob?'

'That's perfectly all right, Mum.'

The sound of many feet scrunching on the gravel next day led Alice to the top window. Instead of the infrequently passing figures in black and children in pairs in and out of the nearby barns on occasion, Alice saw an army approaching. In dark coats of grey or navy or bottle green and wearing hats of different or matching shades, young men and women were coming down the farm drive intently. Some of the women had prams with the hoods up and several of the men pushed wheelbarrows piled high with wooden boxes. It did look like an invasion. Who had asked them to come to see her? Alice walked slowly down the back stairs but heard no sounds in the house. The army of civilians wasn't coming in, so where were they on her land?

The evacuee children were in class so as not to see the setting up, but Alice, upstairs, found a window from which she could see everything. It was a busy scene and all on her best front lawn. Folding wooden trestle tables were carried from her own home it looked like, so Bob must have had quite a lot in a dry barn, and on the tables, spread round the lawn, went the contents of the wooden boxes. Coats came off as the crowd warmed up to their work and Alice got up to see them as they stood around at a tea break.

'He's set up a Fête, he has. The crafty young man. He never told me this yesterday.'

From her high vantage point, Alice saw the cakes appear from tins that the ladies had in their canvas bags. The wellie boot throwing stall was right in her line of sight. She could almost see herself taking a running jump at it. Other stalls were more difficult to guess at. One would be a Tombola and one would be a counting game with sweets in a jar. What was it all in aid of? The air raid practice of the previous week gave her the answer. It must be for the War effort.

Down below, beneath her gaze, small, colourful figures in floral dresses moved around on paths of sunlight, so it seemed to her. The men and a few boys, with jackets off and braces visible, were going to and fro with boxes as quick as she had ever seen anything happening on her lawn. Quicker still came the bunting. Alice had been framing the scene in the shape of her upstairs window, but, in a trice, as she must have looked away, the red, white and blue triangles were waving from stall to stall as if they had always been there and that the front lawn, with its view of the river and the village, was the way to victory.

Alice was wearing a thick knit cardigan over a dress and thought it would be warm enough for the sunny day she could see down there. The breeze from the river might be hardly noticeable with all those people. As she checked that the buttons were done up securely, Alice's final glance before her descent brought her a view of a small wind band making its way to a dais set up by the outer flower beds. On the way down those back stairs, the music began and it brought Alice to a standstill.

'Jack would have loved this. He always liked Tea dances.'

She came down the stairs slowly. Her husband jumped the steps in twos and sometimes threes, cursing always that he couldn't get to a job quickly enough or that Cracky had taken to drink again.

Out in the fresh air, just as she had shed the warmth of the farmhouse and her lively thoughts, Alice was distinctly alone. The garden lawn was behind a high hedge with a gate. It lay beyond her there. Would what she had viewed above make sense from below?

Alice entered and stood by the steps up to the lawn. There was no-one nearby. The music, the running, the shouting were all above her and she made her shuffling steps up towards them, her slippers quite secure on the grass and her ears already tuned in expectation.

Gemma was with one of two camera crews about to circle the garden as the Fête progressed. The evacuee children were going from stall to stall spending their money, and were meeting the strangers in their vintage clothing. No-one was misbehaving.

'Oh heck,' said Gemma to the cameraman. 'Look. She's come out to watch.'

'Is that Bob's mother?' was the reply. 'She looks authentic enough to me.'

It was quite true. Alice's floral print dress and grey cardigan were quite in keeping with the company and her feet were well hidden in the badly maintained lawn.

'Let her be.'

Gemma had to keep watch for the twelve evacuees, so it was no trouble to make sure that Alice wasn't on camera shot for too long.

Alice wandered. Her caution looked like intense interest and this eventually became happy absorption in the scene. She knew what to say.

'How much are you asking for those cakes?'

'I'm not quite up to this game.'

Then came the nudge. It was at the sweet stall quite near where the band was playing, but Alice heard quite clearly.

'I haven't got any pennies left.'

It was one of the boys she had seen lining up in the yard. His trousers weren't very secure in their braces.

Alice's hand went to the pocket of her old print dress and felt some coins. They would be the right ones.

And they were. Alice gave the boy two pre-war pennies and he looked at her with gratitude.

'Thanks a lot, Missus,' came a cockney voice as the band music rose above any conversation and Alice turned to make her way back to her home.

'Get yourself what you want, son.'

She turned into the porch, passing the many wellington boots and stepping over some cabling. Her farmhouse was always such a busy place.

Leopard hides

'Her name's Sonia, and she'll do you proud.'

'I've got to trust to that, then. I have to get her on side.'

'You have, Lep and you'll do it. You've got a way with the girls.'

Lep looked around Roger's place. 'Poppa's Parlour' was his name for it. A lacy lady's bangle of a tattoo on swelling upper arms would be Sonia, he knew it. In the gloom, spotlighted only by the working tattooist, there was not a lot to imagine. The stencils other customers chose were either very small, a morning's work, or upper-body blocks, taking a couple of months. His work was enduring and its timescale lengthy.

'Tell Sonia about the first place you used, Lep. She'll want to know.'

It was true, the very beginning, the starting it all up, was worst of all. There was nothing later to compare with it. Lep had chosen so carefully, too. It was called 'Vector Tattoos', a nicely oblique title on a small shop off a narrow lane in Norwich.

'I'd like a spot of leopard skin.'

'You what?'

'I've got the idea that I'd like them all over.'

'You mad, or something? It'd take forever and you'd never look like the real thing, anyway.'

Lep had turned away and recalled how he had looked around the place as he left. The buttoned, dark leather chairs, the adjustable lamps, a small one-armed bandit in the centre of the room, three tattooists with arms folded to exclude a client who didn't fit in. Norwich wasn't wide-eyed enough.

Whitby served him much better. There was the whiff of sea leading to at least some unknowns. There were dips and views and a background of wild to a wind-swept town quite busy enough to enfold and ignore a man like Lep, who had lived the world over in his time. Up on the surrounding hills, wolves had once roamed, but never a leopard. Lep would hide, anyway. He didn't want to rove and flaunt. His camouflage was his own.

'I get the cat-print idea, but it's a tall order to be the whole animal.'

Sonia didn't look like a reader of 'National Geographic' and neither did Lep. With all the oddity of circumstance and its need of a full customer service, they seemed immediately to meet on the same terms.

'There's no point, otherwise,' said Lep. 'I didn't have any tattoos in the Army, so there's nothing to cover up. Over to you.'

Sonia was looking at stencils as Lep spoke. Tattooing is confrontational enough without staring down the client.

'I know this is different,' Lep continued. 'I'm not customised. What ideas are you looking for there? Start with a spot of yellow, saffron. What've you got? You'll have that dark chestnut grey, won't you?'

'For you, we've got to plan the all-over effect. It's down to you and how long you stay each time. If I'm the one with the first spot, I might not be working on the last.'

'I'm not staying too far away. I've got a pal's cottage about three miles from town and I bus in.'

'When's the last bus?' Sonia was thinking of pace.

'What's that got to do with it? I ain't thinking of sitting here all day. My backside'd rot.'

'Our chairs aren't like that, you can see for yourself. I was only wondering if you'd need to come back some days after a break for lunch.'

These logistics and a great many more to come, taxed them both in the early days.

'Keep a diary, Lep.'

'No. I'll have the job done when and if I can. You ought to know I'm double-booking your two chairs. I'm not having anyone in this room while I'm in it, except you.'

That meant a conversation with the owner.

'It's never been done before. I could lose custom.'

'You won't. How could they know? You won't lose money that's for sure.'

'If you're paying double, there's some might think you want special service, but you won't, you know. We are what we are here. Sonia's so good at it. You'd scarce get better.'

The two men thrashed out an agreement. Two and a half hours minimum every other morning, Monday, Wednesday, Saturday and a week off per month to assess.

The beginning was as big an anticlimax as Lep anticipated. He wasn't a man of raised hopes, nor of dashed illusions. He occupied middle ground, the perennial plain. He had Sonia occupied in the centre, his chest.

'Get started round the nipples, dearie. If I can take that, I can take anything.'

'If we pan out from the chest, it'll work out well.'

It was Lep's decision. He would get to know Sonia by looking up at her from flat on his back. Later, it would be flat on his front, Sonia invisible and unknowable.

It began. The sensation unremarkable in many ways. Lep had been on patrols in parts of Africa where pain and fear went hand in hand. An Army training never quite took away its own reasoning, to be readied for pain and fear.

At least Sonia was feeling for him.

'This is the area covered by a good, thick, bullet-proof top for when the chips are down.'

'That'd be bulky, then?'

'Didn't think about it really.' He couldn't tell Sonia how much he did think about being shielded like that, a human shield. She worked neatly across his bare chest, drawing carefully.

'Take a look now, Lep.' Sonia held a mirror on his chest at an angle to his chin. He craned his neck to look down at the black, cream and saffron damson-sized shapes, creating the close fur of the animal he had chosen to live with, and a smile creased his tightened face muscles.

'Swell. More of the same this session.' Lep lay back as he spoke, his head on a thin pillow. There was nothing of that kind when he had been flat on his back, wriggling under fencing, barbed wire, precarious walls.

His helmet did the shaving along the sandy soil, his neck moved with the rhythm of his hips shifting, his eyes opened really wide to accept the worst.

'Here goes, then,' said Sonia.

It took three months to tattoo the top half of Lep's chest. Sonia varied the task, taking on her days of other customers, diffident and arrogant alike, generally much younger than Lep, but needing a statement all the same. Whitby was anchor land. The sea there blew in its own northern endeavours which had reached right up to the Polar ice in days gone by.

'You love the sun, then?'

It was a chill November day outside at the time. 'Poppas' was warm. There was low background music. It was 10 am.

'When this is done, I'm leaving here.'

'Off to the Bahamas, are you?' Sonia was working around Lep's navel ready to fit the swirl of the spots to meet up at the waist. There are creases around those jerked areas where belts sit, hands delve in to pull and twist all day and every day when sand blows in. How many times does a waist shift and tighten for the military life?

'No, but I've done time in Africa. Never even saw a bloody leopard where I was.'

'You're making up for it now, are you?'

'I suppose I am. These spots'll be all over, like the sun warms you all over. That's the idea. I'm going north.'

'It ain't warm there, I do know that,' Sonia said to the stretched stomach muscles of this thin, military man, as she bent over. 'When it's all done you ain't gonna wear no clothes, are you?'

Lep was looking up at the ceiling, sun bed pose, his tee-shirt pulled up to his armpits.

'I might very well. Your work needs showing off, Sonia.'

'Maybe, but you'll see it in the shower.'

'I'm not going to places where they are.' He saw Sonia shiver. 'I'll be swimming in rivers, though.'

Sonia took it as teasing as she pricked and coloured on the flesh covering taut muscles, only released when she got Lep up to look.

'Very realistic. What do you think?'

Lep's waist and stomach were joined with the diagonal lines of the closely coloured spots, spaced just enough to see flesh which would be pink when the reddening from the procedure had gone down. The sleek look had begun. Lep viewed from a right-angle the folding of the leopard's skin, the underbelly of the animal he would create himself.

Lep's every other days were quite differently spent to Sonia's. Her day off was a Thursday. That day Lep did accounts. Rent was due on Fridays, then there were tattooing fees, Sonia's tips, a bit of decent booze and food. He mostly called in a pizza to keep things simple, but when this was all over, things would be simpler still. He would tie up the accounts and be off.

'North, Lep? That's not leopard territory. You're not really thinking of north from here? It's cold enough already.'

Sonia was referring to a monstrous January of a day outside then. The rain should have been snow. It was viciously sleeting in from a high sea and as it poured down it seemed to tip itself up again, shrouding the town and its air of mystery with nothing more than clammy, freezing fog.

'I really like this sort of weather. I've had it with the heat of Africa. I want the opposite.'

Lep never shivered during the tattoo process. This morning, Sonia had shown him one of the prints for the widest part of his legs, back and below the buttocks. To help the creasing, Lep was up on all fours, crouched, and he had kept his wind-cheater jacket on to 'firm him up a bit'. Sonia's words. His tattooed arms, all achieved over a busy Christmas period, were hidden in the jacket sleeves. Sonia had tied back her long, black hair to begin. Lep had stipulated that both top legs were to be the same and the mirroring work had begun.

'Are you going up the coast, then? Aberdeen?'

'I'm considering the west coast, maybe an isle in a Loch that way.'

'That'll be even more wind and wet. You'd be so exposed.'

'I'll cover up if need be.'

'You've never said why you want all this done. Me and Roger haven't liked to ask. I think we were certain you wouldn't answer.'

Sonia had never been so forthcoming. Aside from the mugs of coffee and the odd bottle of water pushed his way, she had been as unobtrusive as a barber or hairdresser, making the comment on the weather last a morning or the football all an afternoon. There's a pith in the angularity of comments of that kind. This was quite a new departure. It was personal to Sonia.

'I don't know if I'd even get the right answer to give you.'

Bent on all fours as he was to make this reply, Sonia didn't pursue it. Chat is one thing, prying quite another. Anyway, it was obvious to her. The whole-body thing was camouflage, like his flak-jacket in Africa, to make him feel he had a kind of uniform. That's why it had to be all over him. She worked on.

'Of course, it could be I'm getting fond of you.'

'Lep, I'd be right up your 'you know where' if I thought that.'

Flat talk, dismissed from the mind. Pub talk, claptrap.

'That's it, Lep. You can get up now.'

From his crouching position, Lep leant back on his haunches to release his muscles gradually and to undo the pain of a process which was proving interminable. Not Buddha-like, genuflected, at prayer, but a pose all about spring and dexterity and, with a gun in hand, the way to hide in scrub or scree, long grass or razed buildings.

'Stand down for the mirror, Lep. I think you'll like it.'

There was still another leg to tattoo. Time on the couch exactly like today to be re-enacted, but then, so much time was like that, very much the same.

There was a bottle of champagne brought in by Roger for the day when Lep would cease to be his most frequent and highest paying customer. Sonia's family came to view what she had done and to look at this circus act of a wild animal she had created. Her mother had no words for what she saw.

Under a bright light, she saw Lep having a few photographs taken by the local Press. He was wearing a skimpy pair of black underpants, sitting on the couch with one knee raised and back bent to show off the patterning. She knew her daughter to be careful and artistic. She'd seen the tracings, strange ones sometimes, intended for particular parts of a body's hollows. For one young man, she knew Sonia had tattooed a spider web on both of his unusually hollow cheeks. The high cheekbones gave the impression of cave openings, and downright weird, too.

'Classy, yeah?' was Lep's reply to the photo shoot, then, 'Cheers!' He'd be a teetotal from here on.

Sonia stood beside her art work. She raised her glass to Lep.

'Done!'

'Yeah. Done.' Lep lifted his flute to drink and his eyelids came down as he emptied the glass. Tattooed bright blue-green as a leopard's hunting stare, they appeared to cower the room. Those who were watching saw the naked man, unseeing, blotting out his audience, but eager to bow.

They had to clap.

Attached

'Got it, Mum. Settle down now.'

The daughter jumped up from one of the side lamp tables in the restaurant. Being slim, she had judged it right. A light bubbling noise soon resumed.

'Plenty to choose from. Look at this menu. It's completely changed from when we were here last. Do you remember the glazed carrots?' Hetty was reminding her mother that this was a country restaurant of more than local acclaim.

Hetty must have been a student when they last ate here. Her mother tried to nod her thoughts and the effect of time over to the young woman, who came round to adjust her mother's seat forward to the table. The black handbag contraption sat alongside.

'I'm not sure I'll get through it all, but I'll give it a good go,' her mother said quaintly enough. Perhaps even the presentation of the food would oblige with its soft edge, plate-hugging refinement, partnered to entice with as well-judged an amount of very good ingredients as possible. She wondered about beetroot purée.

'What else, Mum? Are you comfortable?'

Reading the menu, however brief and classy it might be, stops all conversation at the level of pomposity. She'd have sounded silly saying 'lemon sorbet plaice goujons' in hospital that same morning. There it was Chef's Choice - Fish cobbler pie, a dish she only tried once. Choice - chosen for you to be good for you. It couldn't hope to replicate this charmed sense of wonder in a fine dining restaurant. For all the experience might disappoint, it begins with a panache of the sort found only on the Continent, if rather crudely translated to these barnacled Isles.

A waiter hovered. They had to read the Wine List and Hetty moved a bulbous wine glass of sparkling water towards her mother.

'This is best for you, after all you've been through. It's incredible that we've got you this far.'

She knew what to do, this daughter, worried as she had been by the earlier mis-diagnosis, attempting to prompt her mother's recovery with this celebratory nod to past occasions. 'You've got through.'

Mother looked down again at the menu. All the inadequacies of kind nurses were still flowing around her dispirited body. She hadn't slept through so many chilly nights as in this August, of all times of the year to fall ill so suddenly. Someone had come and had pulled up the thinnest of blankets to her ears.

'They wouldn't know you if they saw you now, Mum. You were right about that jacket. That's one you'd often choose.'

That was the idea, to get back to a normality which had been taken for granted before the emergency stay in Hospital. It was to ease thoughts of shivering nights and rising temperatures, looking for sleep as if it was guaranteed, but that she had missed the small print.

'What have you chosen? I'm having herring because you always liked it when you came up to Uni to see me. It's served with horseradish and they'll do that brilliantly here. I'm following it with salt beef and minted pea salad. That'll nourish. What about you, Mum?'

A starched table cloth pressed on her lap as she leaned back to deliver the answer to the question. In order to get through this she would have to get started.

'What about the flaked haddock rosti? It'll be strong flavours. Do you good, Mum.'

Hetty wasn't anxious, but forthcoming. Her mother was the capable woman only temporarily cut down a size or two by the operation.

This was choice food to choose. On their many double dining occasions, they'd always had interesting and varied selections.

'I may have the calves liver with the fancy bubble and squeak. I have to get my strength up.'

'Yes, and get out more, Mum, like this. Things to do are good for you.'

'You're the best for me, Hetty. This is a lovely idea.'

The little ways of the numerous nurses who played by her recovering world in that side room, swept into her mind and left her wondering about the edges we pick at when we take on other people's lives. Like the food about to be delivered on the plates to them both, the items carefully arranged, Nurses had circled around her, concentrating on that centre point, so stilled, hurting badly, pampered with monitored attention and she eager to please with little or no strength to do so.

Hetty ordered and made it clear to the waiter about the wine. They would stay with water with good reason.

It was the staple of the bedside table, the plastic jug of water. If nurses saw an empty beaker, they filled it with all the anticipation of enabling a life-giving force.

'This you must have, above all else,' and they were right, provided the hand could lift a cup, aim for the mouth and enjoy. Of course, there was always time to feel the effect. Time stretched out to a goodness meant to be as beautiful as watching a stream. In between the sleeping, the watching was all. The patterning of a notice board, an alarm button too high, the window blinds open or shut and all at the whim of a committee or a busy nurse circling, always circling in good or bad dreams, attempting to do good.

'It's such a treat to have this, isn't it, Mum?' The plates had arrived and the dishes served from a trolley. An impeccably dressed pair posed very professionally beside her. They looked down at her feet.

'I'm managing quite well. I'll have a few mushrooms with this, that's all,' she said as a napkin was placed on her lap. It was a whole quarter of the size of the tablecloth and starched stiffly enough to walk away on its four corner points.

The cream plastic Hospital tray glided above her, bearing the fruits of doing well. It was swivelled round expertly in its place over her tummy area by a nursing assistant, skilled as yet in nothing but a cheery smile. She was left alone once with a banana and her one good hand. A hundred ideas of how to tackle it came to her before her scarcely focussing mind invited a monkey into the room to help.

'It's always tender when they flake haddock, isn't it? It's easy to poach it solid if you don't watch what you're doing.' Hetty was about to pour some more sparkling water for her mother. They had waved away the attentions of the trolley and their two dishes glowed. Hetty's herring fillet was curled over to show its turtle dove colouring of pinks, browns and greys. It was bedded in lettuce and a flecked horseradish sauce.

'You should have this, Mum. You'll remember that trip to Amsterdam.'

'Yes, I would. What marinade have they used?'

Hetty cut a soft slice of the raw fish. 'Oh, wine vinegar, definitely. Now, what about yours?'

For such a small amount of food, it seemed a deal of conversation for the flake or two of haddock she had chosen. Hospital menu fish, generally battered, was a Friday penance, if batter could be considered as such. There was very little flake of any sort within the foamy shell she had been served one day. Now a tender forkful balanced lightly enough and there was nothing else to look at except itself.

'They put it with the rosti to prove that they can soften the fish and match textures. Is that your impression?' Hetty never wavered from her mother 'doing well', and learning to enjoy all these firsts over again.

After critical care, her nurses never came into the room to spy on her but to aid a process. This was their training over and above the specialisation. They praised the gains made, erring on the dismissive when the shivers came or the temperature rose, saying:- 'I'll get the doctor to look in on you'. Otherwise they paraded praise, much as this meal did, every mouthful a step forward into that new post-operative life swell.

Hetty was toying with lettuce. Every curl looked lively, twirling a sense of adequateness into each mouthful. These beauties were rather well-oiled, ready for confident digestion.

It was confidence she craved, gained slowly from that first lift out of the bed onto the floor. She had tested it gently with toes unused to solid floor for a week or two and quite difficult to see when she couldn't bend too well.

'The more you do, the more you will want to do,' must have been a Physiotherapist's snappy phrase.

'I'd really like more of this,' said Hetty to herself. 'What do you think, Mum? How's the taste?'

'Oh, perfect. They have got it right like you said.'

'I knew they would. They would for you, anyway. They can see how you are placed.' Hetty's knife and fork came onto the plate. A smidgeon of marinade stayed on the silvered knife blade.

Hetty picked up a dainty roll from her side plate and applied butter while looking up at her mother.

'I'll butter yours for you. They'll soon be here with the main.'

Waiting for service, then digestive juices, then friendly arms to help you slipped down in the bed after failing completely with packaged cheese and biscuits. Her saviour had been a Nurse on duty for over twelve hours. What was a cellophane packaging to all the medicines and dressings she had opened?

'Yes, go ahead. I'd just be extra slow.'

'That's the last thing to worry about. Take your time. It'll mean you've made way for dessert.'

In Hospital she had been told that some patients put food to one side for later, for when they felt up to it. This meal had to be a complete whole, as if she had reclaimed her whole life, forced again to be that former woman, sitting intently, talking with animation and yes, explaining herself. Here the meal was an explanation, the key to the next and the next.

The dessert possibilities proved to be fantastic this evening. Hetty was most impressed.

'This is a whizz. Remember that surprising restaurant in mid-Wales, when we picked up on an end of evening glut of food? The Chef had been experimenting all day.'

Hetty had remembered foams and sorbets of all sorts presented at Machynlleth. How unlikely a place for lightweight tempting confections in Disneyworld colours when the family was making its way to the grey mountains. The possibilities were not like that in her distant Hospital room. She stayed with the unsurprising staples, hoping that rice pudding was staple enough.

'Mum,' came Hetty's voice. 'Pistachio doughnut'. What next?'

She chose chocolate medley. How many times had she wanted that creamy texture on her tongue in all those long days. All she queried from her Hospital stay was the insistence on the return to normal, the radical equipping for the resumption of living when she was so constrained.

'Perfect, don't you think, Mum? They do know how to pamper here. I've said we'll have to pass on coffees. It'll take a while to tease you out of your chair. I'll get you unplugged at the wall.'

The black handbag sat heavily on the floor beside her. All the while she had been attached to this pulsing vacuum pump, taking away the final evidence of infection. It was a portable appliance now, when in previous years it had been as large as a freezer, they told her on the ward.

'That's it, Mum.' Hetty stood up and shook back her hair after the crawl to the skirting board socket. 'I'll put this carefully on your lap so that we can go. We've had a very good time, haven't we?'

The Unloved

'What do you mean, empty frames? You're a jerk.'

It buzzed through Thomas's head. 'No, not a jerk. I really have got a good idea and it'll work, I know it will.'

Anitya nudged his arm. 'You're not here to make things work. We're only part time, remember?'

Thomas had got used to this blunt student from Kiev.

'Anitya, I've got ideas. Not so many people have ideas. I can speak to Management and see it through.'

'Empty frames. You'd see through them!' Anitya laughed with Thomas and clapped him on the back.

The two of them were in the rear rooms of a Charity shop in Chichester. It was just off the High Street along a road of cafés, late night restaurants and gift shops. It stood in a good area and recent donations had been up.

'I've got the idea for a zany event. All the mismatched frames we've ever had could find a good home.'

'Yes, there are plenty for firewood. People will ask, 'What sort of frames, spectacle frames?' How could we just use frames, especially the empty ones?'

'It's the empty ones which are best. Mostly we get bad reproductions or foxed pictures which need to come out, and the frames don't often improve the picture in it. That's why they're here, but hardly anyone reaches down to pick up a bargain out of the boxes. They're always on the floor for safety with the glass. There'd be hundreds parked in all our shops.'

'There would be, but so what? Not many people buy frames. Why should they?'

'That's just what we have to think through. With my idea we could get realistic prices for the dullest and even auction the very best.'

"Antiques Roadshow', with just frames? We'd look like freaks. Got it! 'Freaky frames'!'

'No, you're the jerk now!' Thomas gave his companion a nudge. 'We need an upmarket image, like when we do the clothing Floor Shows and get the catwalk models. I'd like the chance to hang all the unloved frames on the walls of a small warehouse. Plenty of parking space and a low premium for an evening let. What d'you think?'

'I think we can't show just empty frames. The sort we get wouldn't glitter or glow or look vintage or cherished, they'd just look arrrgh...'

'But they needn't. We could be arty and display them in a way that draws the eye. Empty frames could have an interesting new item in, wallpaper patterns, a ticket or a concert programme, put there with blu-tack once the frames were arranged.'

Thomas's ideas took on a fascination against all the odds.

'Wouldn't the frames look very tiny and lost in a large space?'

'Yes, unless we grouped them in fours or sixes or eights, depending on the quality and type we got. One minivan load is all we'd need to get on with.'

'You'd want drinks on a centre table. How would they buy? You'd wait until the end, I suppose, like the dress shows?'

'Maybe, and I've got another idea. I know someone who lectures on Art. What if he could give a talk on framing the great masters, or how frames are constructed? Behind the scenes stuff, you know.'

'We don't want lectures, though, do we?'

'No, but someone who knows their stuff, we do.'

Thomas and Anitya had been sorting through all the while they chattered. They had hung up belts, thrown shirts into one box, trousers in another, a hurly burly of the usual morning at the back of the shop. Their ideas took them into promotional thinking, the province of the Manager.

Her response was quite predictable.

'Impossible. We haven't got the resources.' Delia delivered her sentence.

'We haven't in this shop, Delia, but across the county we'd pull in a lot of interest.' Thomas stood by the till surrounded by the jarring colours of the locals' bric-a-brac.

'Well, go up a level, then. I've got Stan Maidment's email address, but he'll need a comprehensive plan. I know him, he'll only move when he's tickled or pushed.'

'I'll sort it then, Delia,' said Thomas with the kind of conviction Delia liked to hear in her volunteers.

Dorchester proved a pivotal centre for the County's volunteers. Stan had replied with a cautious 'yes' and met up with Thomas within the month.

'Some things are simple and other things are quite difficult,' he said cheerily to begin. 'Getting the frames together is as easy as pie. Hanging them is the job of an artist, or they'll just look a mess.'

'Anitya and I think we've worked that one out. With the right kind of planning we'd group all the types. I've got a local framing shop ready to help.'

'That's good publicity for them. Well done, but then it's the sorting. Where is the manpower coming from, Thomas?'

'I've got family in on it. Anitya's got some friends together. They're all from parts of Russia originally, or Ukraine, and they know about The Hermitage.'

'Remind me,' said Stan, stirring his coffee to produce a frothy glaze.

'Turned out, she says, that during the Siege of Leningrad, the Museum had to store all its masterpieces and they were sent over to Siberia. The frames were left on the walls in place.'

'So?' Stan was after facts.

'The staff were unpaid, of course, but they showed visitors around still, telling them what had been on the walls, in the empty frames.'

'And starving, like as not. What an idea. Can you get a photo from a website? I'll fund its enlargement and we'll put it in the entrance area. That'll set the scene, Thomas, of what can be done with empty frames.'

Thomas looked at Stan with a broad smile.

'Can you fund a few other ideas? Anitya's keen on some hands-on activities in the same large room as the showing, like we're interpreting what the punters could do with the frames. She thinks a gilder could give a demonstration on distressing paint. I know it'd be more fuss, but if we have add-ins, we'd be sure of a larger audience.

'What else, then?'

'I'm not wanting to take away from the big display itself because that ought to impress, but after a walk around, our buyers would want to talk to anyone with an interest in framing'

'Okay, you've got a Framer coming. Will they bring examples of what can be achieved? Remember, it's all the other way round for them. The frame comes first. We don't provide the art work, right?'

'That's right. All our frames will be empty, except for a buttonhole centre in some of them. Anitya thinks shells, buds, playing cards, postcards. You know, they'd be small objects just to develop an interest and not in every one of them, either. We want the empty frames to speak for themselves.'

'And what more?'

'I think we need an Art Historian on hand. I wouldn't know who. Someone who'll bring books to show great paintings in the fancy frames of an Art Gallery. They could be put up with the visual from the Hermitage Museum. It'd be great set up beside the big photo of those empty frames.'

'It's just producing another thing to look at, Thomas. We've got to concentrate on purchase.'

'Yes, well, hands on varnish and paint stripping. How to change a frame to your advantage, that sort of thing, we'd get from a couple of Anitya's friends.'

'That's what we want then, practical stuff for the target audience. I can see small frames as mobiles, upgraded light wood with twinkly things in, or hearts. You know the kind of thing. A craft product.'

Thomas was leaning forward across their small table. 'Can we all meet up with you? Have you got the time to flesh things out?'

'I'll make the time. Email me the options and I'll get back to you.'

Thomas made the decision to visit the Dorset Charity shops himself.

One after the other, shop by shop over the next few weeks, he went down on his haunches to count and assess the frames in the boxes on the floor. Customers ignored him and squeezed by. The counter staff were more forthcoming.

'We've got more than we ever put out. They're rubbish really.'

'I didn't realise we had so many. They don't sell, I don't think.'

'Exhibit them? Funny idea. Who'd pay to look at empty frames?'

'You can have them all and welcome. That'd clear the floor space.'

Thomas reported to Anitya.

'We'd get hundreds if not a thousand, at the drop of a hat. I haven't found one shop where they'd not be thankful to be rid of them. They're just clutter.'

'We'll make clutter a buyer's premium. I've got Petyor to take some classy photographs. I painted a few and he arranged them for a flier photo.' She held up her iPad and the screen glowed with a criss-cross of natural wood frames, flanking a brass one in the centre.

'Old and new, that's good.'

The other photographs were also eye-catching. Anitya's friends had captured the spirit of the enterprise. Art, craft and a bit of magic had answered a lot of questions about dull, unloved frames.

'This'll take off once we've seen Stan. You've got the practical ideas he wanted. He didn't fancy the History talks, so we'll put the Photographer and Framer to him. Is your friend aiming to become a professional?'

'We all aim for that, Thomas, don't you?

Stan saw to every aspect of publicity.

'If we're doing it, we've got to tell everyone. The charity stakes are always high on the agenda. I've got the Mayor agreeing to open the event. She's used her influence and they're getting one of the best oil paintings of a mayor to add to our selection. The man in charge is ours for the day, she says, because he has to remove it when we shut up shop. He'll help to hang with all the others.'

Around the two volunteers, the programme for the event took shape. Photographer and Framer saw it as a good business pitch without making their display look like a drab Business Fair. The empty frames would be more than a day's work in the hanging on the vast pin boards hired in.

'Put a few in a box underneath each presentation space,' Thomas said. 'Let's remind everyone where they all originate - unloved donations.'

The warehouse floor was in good condition as a carpet firm had recently moved out. The lighting was harsh, but for empty frames that hardly mattered. There were no pictures to be spoiled by the glare. Instead, all round the walls on a dove-grey backing, creations built up by volunteers during that day, glowed in their own right. Thomas's original idea was now in a third dimension, glinting on grey walls, angling differently at every step and inviting inspection. Photographs of the volunteers beside their own frame creations were taken for the local Newspaper and the Charity's website. Thomas's momentum had been achieved and Stan came up to him several times during the evening.

'Our sticker system is working, just like it would on pictures costing hundreds in an Art shop. Empty frames, though, Thomas, empty frames. They're selling well.'

The oddity of the enterprise, billed on the fliers as 'You've been framed - a new-look Charity Event', intrigued people from the county and beyond. There was just enough car-parking space and, if you were looking at the makes of cars, enough money in every punter's pocket.

Delia came up to Thomas about half an hour before the viewing time was up. There would be a rush for her volunteers then.

'Unbelievable. We've had donated frames brought in, and even those have been stickered in the boxes on the floor.'

'We've had about enough up on the walls, I think, Delia. I've spoken to a Hairdresser. He's stickered almost fifty frames for a new design in his salon. He said something about shades of grey and showing off his dye treatments with curls in the frames.'

'Oh, did he?' laughed Delia, and saw the Mayor approaching as she did so.

'Lady Mayor, let me introduce you to our ideas man, Thomas. He was the one with the original inspiration.'

Mrs. Bartlett was in full dress, just like her namesake in the oil-painting on the wall near to where she had been sitting.

She walked away with Thomas.

'You got this many to come for Charity on just a single idea? We could do with more volunteers like you.'

Thomas was looking closely at her mayoral chain as she turned to him. The time for counting stickers was due and he had to go.

'How did the idea come to you?'

'I saw a couple of boxes on the floor of our shop and I went over to tidy them up one day. The frames were all different shapes, caught in a jumble and difficult to pick up and see what you had actually got. They were the most unloved items in the shop, in all our shops, on the floor in cardboard boxes.'

Mrs. Bartlett seemed prepared to let him go. 'Cardboard boxes?'

Her remark clearly followed him as he turned.

'There are plenty of things left around in them. People for instance.'

In the Home

Aggie sat comfortably enough. There was a glass of water at her elbow and her feet were raised on a small stool because her ankles had recently shown signs of swelling. The television was on in the Day Room.

Benny checked his notes for the day and Aggie nodded to this Care Assistant just as all the others did, glad of company, safe in sure hands. There was not a lot more movement unless they called out and Aggie wasn't one of those.

Around Benny was all the paraphernalia of a Care Home, sitting as comfortably as it could in a glare more suitable to Office premises. No dark could be enjoyed during the day. The elderly couldn't be expected to cover their faces with a shawl as might be done in the Mediterranean against the hot sun on lined, old faces. If they dozed it was with the glare of a bright room on their eyelids, not felt, but known until drowse became sleep and only they to know the difference on that milky way into darkness.

Acacia Court had gone for light grey furnishing, the colour of some computer plugs. A hint of red and brown squeezed through the ranks of chairs where an autumn tweed spread its spoil on a bed of concrete. Splashes of art work on the walls were consistently of flowers and any colour suited the walls painted pale Wedgwood blue.

'I'll get your hot drink this morning as usual.'

The something he felt he had to say caught Benny by surprise. He spoke because Aggie had moved slightly in her chair. He saw it out of the corner of his eye. It was not a movement as if she had felt a twinge and shifted. It was staged and very self-conscious, almost as thought about as taking a sip of tea. That takes concentration.

'I'll look forward to it,' was said in reply.

Benny moved on. The corridor with rooms off was wide for good reason but suited more to a warehouse deck despite the florals along it. A wall art clock shaped as Old Father Time was displayed in the corridor lay-by with its easy chairs for guests. He shared an Office with Sue. She was local, he from Poland and together they managed the day to day running of the Home. The elderly were mostly eager to adapt to strangers with any sort of accent, local or European, as long as they brought them their tea.

'Can't tell what's going to happen when we get the Inspection.'

'It's over to management, not us,' Sue clicked out from a mouth full of biscuit. She swallowed it.

The two of them settled to what constituted a break, something to say across a table when it isn't like home, nor a cafeteria with friends. The elbows are more taut on the table, the crumbs have to go further.

At tea break the two of them supervised the trolleys delivered by trainee assistants or volunteers. Benny was on Day Room duty, usually an idling of time punctuated with well-paced, nuanced, well-intentioned cries at some volume from the various volunteers.

'How do you want your tea this morning, Mavis?'

'All right for your usual, Peter?'

Benny was on hand for propping up, shoving in a cushion or two, positioning the cup or mug. When he got to Aggie, she was as alert and as bright-eyed as ever.

'Nicest part of the day this. You know you're safely through the night.'

'Oh, yes, but you've had breakfast?'

Aggie looked up at him.

'That's too many fingers and thumbs. I like tea when it's on its own.'

'How do your ankles feel, Aggie?'

'Oh, about right. How long do I have to keep them up during the day, d'you think? I have them up all night, don't I?'

'You'll get a check on them at the end of the week.'

Benny left later to complete his notes. Ankle checks were weekly and Aggie had been on the list for about a month. After this week he would contact her niece, Phyllis. Aggie's only son was in Australia.

He was in the corridor when he found the anticipated visitor seated in the alcove under 'Old Father Time'.

'Hallo there. Have you been given a coffee? I'm Benny, one of the Care Assistants here. They phoned from Reception.'

The man looked pensively up at him. The broad shoulders of a forty-year old were hunched as if over an invisible magazine.

'I was passing, so I checked in with Reception. I thought I'd call in about my Dad, whether you'd got a place for him or not.'

'I'm not the one who'd know that, but I can show you round. There's time before lunch. What did you say your name was?'

Benny's easy manner worked.

'I'm Matt Lewis and my Dad's name is Charles,' was said as the two men strolled back to the Day Room and passed the kitchens.

'Everything's off this corridor. Breakfast and lunch is served hot, then there's a cold buffet supper because we begin so early, you see.'

'That's what I'm finding with Dad now. He's up so early, like he's got to be ready for a day's work or doesn't like the dark.'

'There's a few like that. The elderly like to repeat a known routine. We notice it often, or there's a relative, much like you, tells us about it because they've lived with it first.'

Coming up to the Day room, Benny let Matt walk in ahead of him and as the bulky man moved over, Benny saw Aggie's stool roll over towards him from her chair nearby. Aggie was slumped in her chair and her heels were placed to point her toes upright. They had come down sharply on the carpet from the stool.

'Stay here, Matt. Have a look round. I'll be with you in a second.'

'Aggie, let's get you comfortable,' he immediately said to her, coming across the short distance from the door.

'I felt it go,' said Aggie, but she made no fuss as Benny moved her back, then lifted her feet onto the uprighted stool.

'That's going to happen, Aggie, so we'll get you a recliner.' Benny spoke with a tone meaning not straightaway. He would get something clear in his mind first. Why was Aggie moving down a chair so purposefully a little space at a time? She wasn't a confused individual and she'd know a stool would go over if she did what she did.

Matt needed to be seen off, so Benny got up and went over to him.

'All part of the service,' he smiled.

As Matt left from the downstairs Reception area, Sue was standing there.

'He wasn't our undercover agent, was he?'

'Don't think so, Sue. He didn't ask those sort of questions. Can I get a recliner from Chair store? How many have we got at the moment?'

'There's a couple, I'm sure. Who are you thinking of?'

'It's Aggie. I'm scared she'll fall off her chair with just a footstool for her legs.'

'She's usually so good and co-operative. I wonder what's up?'

'We'll see if the recliner does the trick.'

He and a volunteer in that afternoon moved the recliner into the Day Room just ahead of the timing of the after-lunch rest.

'Thanks. I'll see she takes to it all right.'

Benny sat to watch the residents wander in to take up position for the second half of their day. It would go on until 7 or 8pm with a cold supper to punctuate the time unless relatives came to take them out. He saw John, a long-retired builder, dressed ready for an outing.

'Is it your brother coming for you, John?'

Quite soon a volunteer was helping Aggie in and Benny got up.

'How's she been? I've got Aggie a new chair to see how it goes with her legs. I told her about it this morning.'

'I'm looking forward to it,' said Aggie to them both. She obviously didn't mind being steered towards a warm red armchair.

The two of them helped her to sit.

'Feel this against the back of your legs, Aggie.'

'That's firm.'

'Now, I press here. You can do it for yourself if you want. It goes slowly.'

Benny watched Aggie's face as her legs were raised to the horizontal and she relaxed. It seemed to be the best thing for her. She leaned onto the upright back and looked pleased.

'This'll suit me very well.'

Benny opted for overtime on the following two days and was scrupulous in his watchfulness. Aggie had made herself look comfortable in the recliner just like a couple of the others, but in mid-afternoons, coming up to the four o'clock mark, she seemed to become frustrated with the arrangement and tried to wriggle down the recliner without letting the leg rest down as a simple button would have enabled her to do.

Benny stood away from her at the side of the room to watch, propping a lap top on a shelf so that he could get ahead with other matters. There was the usual afternoon's-worth of intermittent chat or calling. It was a quiet time. Cleaners came in the mornings and as it was the School run now, they were picking up their children. Benny could hear the muffled sound of a little more traffic passing by. That world scarcely touched this one of quiet thoughts and half doze, but Aggie had set up a different pattern. She shunted forward little by little with movements as if she was on a roller coaster ride and wanted to get off without showing fear. The Dodgems were on her mind, he felt sure, as she moved with her eyes shut, unsure and slightly agitated, awaiting the end of the perilous ride. Benny had never watched like this before. His eyes became the surveillance camera for a recall of what had been occurring.

The niece came at the end of this long week. Benny was on the Office phone confirming rosters for the weekend as he always did.

'Your aunt's pretty well, Mrs. Mayhew. She's just not happy with the recliner we got her on account of her ankles. Maybe she could get back to her easy chair when the medication begins to work.'

'Is it long term, do you think?' Phyllis needed to let Aggie's son know of changes.

'The chair itself isn't doing her any harm, it's the way she uses it.'

Phyllis Mayhew's eyes clouded as Benny briefly described the actions he had watched so closely.'

'She doesn't do this in bed because she's under covers there. It's just the open chair,' was her reply.

'But there's nothing wrong with the chair. We've got several in use.'

'No, I didn't mean that. Can we go and see her? Show me where you stand.'

The two stood shielded by a bookcase at the door of the Day Room. Aggie was opposite them. She had moved down and was raised up on her elbows at the fold in the recliner. Her knees were bent and her feet on the floor at the end.

'Oh dear, that won't do,' said Phyllis, quietly going forward to help. 'She's remembering her childhood, I know.'

'You need your feet up, Aggie. I'm here for a while.'

She was half dozing, but the two of them got Aggie upright, then Phyllis stayed and the afternoon wore on.

Aggie's movements became the same as Benny had witnessed, but he would not have known to say these lines which Phyllis whispered in Aggie's ear very slowly and comfortingly.

'Is he coming? Is he coming? Be brave. He'll go out again this time because you're awake and on the end of the bed. He won't come on your bed tonight. He'll see you sitting upright. Is he gone, Aggie? Yes, he's gone, Aggie.'

Phyllis left her aunt to slip along to Benny's Office.

'I'll be back tomorrow, but my advice is to put a light cover over her when she has to be in that chair, so that she feels secure. Lying down like that must remind her of when she was too frightened to get into bed to sleep when she was a child. It's the trauma of the childhood her own father took away from her.'

Angels are hands-on

Are you off to wash your hands?'

'No, Father, not yet, but there's time enough.'

Oliver's replies were usually more jaunty than this. A reply was absolutely necessary in this potent place.

Oliver had been allocated a room for the year at St. Michael's to study, contemplate, revise.

His Parish Priest had told him that St. Michael's was out of the way enough.

He arrived in a blustery early November from London where his studies were curtailed temporarily by illness. His lungs were weaker than any specialist had thought. Good, fresh air was the advice and Oliver had to take it, making the most of the enforced sabbatical. He helped out in the Retreat Centre attached to St. Michael's Monastery and was meant to do as much or as little as he liked. He could lecture, lead discussion or just wash up.

On the way to his room that day in his first fortnight, Oliver had turned a different corner. He saw numerous doors filing down a grand width of corridor ahead. Anyone who opened opposite doors along it would have to waltz across to shake hands. Light in this unused strait was provided by rectangular glass panes, each one frosted and lettered with the name of a saint above its solid door. Oliver stepped down to investigate and knew what he would find. The dusty holiness of forgotten saints met him as he passed by each door on the right flank and then up again, along the left.

He didn't flinch. The wide corridor did not remind him of school or University, but of some sepia-tinted photographs he had seen of a hospital in an illustrated history of war. The same forced quiet was here, as it seemed the Nurses commanded there, but the beds which would have dominated a sociable space, mopped often, were behind the doors. There, saintly lives were laid on saintly lives.

61

Oliver turned from the empty top corridor to find Bernie waiting for him. He was the Retreat House manager and general do-gooder. He'd been very happy to find Oliver on his doorstep.

'It's been left unused for years, Oliver. Shame, but the guys just aren't out there.'

'They've all gone to wash their hands,' Oliver quipped, as Father was considered expert in the phrase.

'They're away with their hands on something else.' Bernie turned his back on the corridor. 'No-one wants this kind of quiet any more.'

St. Michael's stood, a vast red-brick building with a tower tall enough to be seen for miles in rural Warwickshire. To stand beneath it as Oliver did just after he had left Bernie, was to encompass a new life, within ever-widening circles. He looked up to the flagpole. On windy nights its rope flapped insecurely outside the room allocated to him on the top floor.

'You're out of the way, here,' Father had said on Oliver's arrival.

'I don't mean to be in the way,' was his reply, but he was unprepared for Father's response.

'It's up here the angels can't harm, y'know. Now come down with me and wash your hands.'

Oliver descended a staircase lit by a tall landing window, two high-ceilinged rooms in height, incongruously wide so as to give extra light to pick out the stone flags. They were for stepping out in robe, cassock and good leather shoes worn to shape surfaces not fashioned to be worn down. Pugin knew what he was doing.

At supper that evening a group of six was beginning a mini-Retreat, Friday to Sunday.

'How can you live in a huge place like this without feeling swamped?' It was a Law student from London who spoke.

'I'm living up aloft,' Oliver explained like an old hand. 'Given the scale of this place, I've got a minute room. This table is about as grand as it gets. It's all been pared down to the minimum.'

'How extraordinary it must have been, filled with that sort of stuff from the past.' Keen eyes met Oliver's gaze and a quizzical look formed his answer.

'We have to see it like it is. It's a very different kind of emptiness now. You'll get what I mean when you walk around tomorrow. Take your time and drink it in. This place isn't crowded out like a stuffed museum.'

After supper, Oliver entered that bit of space which St. Michael's gave him. He opened his door and looked up at the window. The brick tower loomed to the left, and he saw its parapet like a strengthening barrel's rim. He felt the buttressing of his room against the bulk of the building, a necessity to the architect and not a neglected corner in any sense. As he coughed and made draughts secure, Oliver sat at the computer desk with a certain glee. What would the tower know of this press-button life, was a fleeting thought.

It was next morning early that Oliver came down from his room for no other reason than to greet the day. It was already well into November and a day takes a while to get going at that time of year. He was on his way to the Chapel, which was the sort of place you did not come across casually.

From the exterior it rose up beside the tower like an inconsequential acquaintance. Both served each other well enough, but it seemed a firm friendship might never be theirs.

He came into the pitch blackness by a side door he knew well. It was his exit when the Retreat groups were being shown around by Father. One light switch here gave him enough of blearness to imagine the early rises of those who formerly used this place. They were not in his shadow. Oliver was on the hunt for angels.

'Whey up, man.' An accented voice was right beside him.

'Okay,' was Oliver's surprising reply.

'Well, I'm not. You're about early?' The query was not meant to produce an answer and Oliver knew it. His leader had been here before him.

'I've come to have a really good look round before it fills up a bit.'

'It's already full,' came the reply.

Oliver stepped forward a few paces and stared at his unbooked tour guide.

Stubble first, on a chin he hadn't seen before, Oliver confronted a caretaker. His jaw jutted purposefully forward. He rolled his eyes and the whites blinked at Oliver like miners' lamps.

'How many are there of us?' Oliver just thought to say as it was indicated that they go forward.

'Wouldn't you like to know,' came the answer from a man facing away from him now.

His working jacket had two folds vertically down to the waist. It was a shiny workaday serge and the well-used creases caught the dim light as the man moved forward.

'We won't put on the lights yet,' the man confided and then turned his black face round to him. 'I'll let the morning show you the glory slowly,' and he shifted into a better shaft of light.

How had Oliver not met him before? A bunch of keys, the badge of a caretaker, hung at his waist and reached down to his knees at different levels like tubular bells. His trousers bulged with filled pockets on each flank and a hand at the end of a long arm played with the keys.

'You'll know better than I do where to go.'

'That's right I do. There's always a way only one person knows.'

He walked towards the aisle of the vast building and Oliver quite suddenly needed to say a name.

'What shall I call you if you're showing me round?'

'Brad's my name.'

The figure moved off into the aisle of the Chapel, pushing a few chairs straight on his way to a candle stand. One lighted candle, just placed and presumably Brad's, glowed childlike and small, but they went right past it round the other side of the pillar. There Brad stopped.

'You're interested in the Angels?'

'Well, our literature says 'St. Michael and all Angels'. Are they all here?'

Oliver's humorous remark only served to make Brad move on with a jerk and clatter of keys which echoed a reply from the Chapel.

Then it was a ceaseless round of 'here', 'there', 'under', 'over', 'above', 'beside' and 'behind', which left Oliver a dazed dreamer awakening after a long night's sleep. The amount of information crowding his head was there for a day or a life, if only it could be processed in those moments of comfort and awe.

Brad must have done this tour before. He had a route, a patter and an expertise which he wore lightly. He strolled, he didn't pace. His long legs and thin shape fitted every corner where the carved and gilded angels lurked. They glowed before Oliver on painted screens, in filigree brass and silvered frames. They were etched in every lamp stand and light fitting. They gazed brightly down from windows and crevices above, oblivious of the morning light revealing only a portion of their glory.

'I never knew there were so many here.' Oliver once offered to Brad, but there was no need for speech. The angels sang.

Brad completed his tour at the High Altar where the immense carvings of two angels kneeling with wings curled over in praise resembled the Tabernacle. There was a light to illuminate their grandeur and cost which Brad switched on.

'What a wow,' said Oliver. This was to be tour's end.

End it was, as Brad moved across to a priest's door and went through it.

Oliver sat down on the altar steps to continue his experience on hard marble. This was the first touch. He had handled nothing and had only gazed. He felt Brad's absence as he sat there under the glare of the light looking up at the Angels' faces brightened so sharply by the Caretaker's click.

Brad had led him to more than one hundred angels in the space of a mere twenty minutes in this uncompromising Chapel space. It felt much more like a walk in a concourse, with people everywhere, like Birmingham New Street when he had guests to collect. The shadows of the crowds were parting for him.

'Are you going somewhere? Is it time to wash your hands?'

The question came out of the blue as Oliver stood up and turned.

'No, Father, but I'll keep them off the angels.'

'I'll walk with you to the tower room. Does it suit?'

'Yes, of course it does.'

'Then you'll stay the year.'

Oliver walked with Father to the door of the Chapel. It was a small door and it had led him to Brad.

'So, what else does Brad do?' said Oliver as he turned to Father O'Connor.

The balding priest pulled at the lapels of his suit and looked at the oak door which Oliver had opened.

'He does what he needs to do. After you, Oliver.'

Principal

'She was one of us, but she wasn't. You know what I mean.'

'I do and I don't. I know she made a great impression on you.'

'Oh, yes, she did, on all of us.'

Patty touched the hair highlighted from its salon treatment the day before with an exactly copied movement of her hairdresser. The full styling bounced.

'She kept herself so well, Tim. Lillian never let herself down over all those years at the College.'

'She had to set an example, I suppose.'

'Too right, she did, and what a role model she was. The blokes knew she'd see to their promotion prospects. That's important, Tim.'

'She was one of those cushioning types. You know you'll fall softly if you fall at all.'

'She never let us think we couldn't achieve. She inspired such confidence in her, the College, the administration. She had her hands on every aspect of things.'

'You were always so happy at the end-of-year bashes.'

'Blissfully. Another good year gone by. She was brilliant.'

Around this pair, time hurried through an extraordinarily busy early retirement. It had slowed to a shocked halt that morning.

'Lillian's gone. The family has sent the funeral date.'

'Oh, I am sorry, Patty.'

'It's to be expected. Just think how long ago it all was, really. She was the Principal for twenty years and I left after fifteen to have John. She was the mainstay of my early career. It really seemed as if nothing could faze her.'

'I remember you saying once that she was part of everyone's family.' Tim eyed the garden as he put on the kettle. A game of golf had been booked for early afternoon.

'She was. She came round when I had John at home for weeks with tonsillitis. I'd left the College then, of course, but I was still one of her first batch of staff.'

Patty took the mug of tea from Tim.

'It'll be a reunion at the funeral.'

''Course it will. That's what they're for.'

And so Patty would meet up with the senders of a sizeable cohort of Christmas cards after so long. Almost every nuance of growing children, their education and marriages along with a decent smattering of grandchildren seeped into her as she thought of those end of term parties with their merry faces. Lillian kept them all going with her wound clockwork spring set for each and every occasion. It seemed never to wind down. Was it all poise? It wasn't posturing. She wore such beautiful clothes, as one who could stretch to afford them and find time to hang them on her as a fine ham needs time for perfection. Lillian was built to last, Patty had thought, and now she was gone.

'Blow that, Tim.'

'What love?'

'I mean blow it. She shouldn't have gone.'

'She's gone her length of years, Patty. You can't ask more than that.'

Patty went to her wardrobe when Tim set off for his game. It had sliding, mirrored doors. She stood to enquire of the mirror.

'What shall I wear?'

If the doors had slid open of their own accord and ejected the right outfit like an advert, she would not have been surprised. She knew already what to wear so as to meet up after all these years. Lillian would approve of a mature choice. Cream and brown, leather belt not too prominent, soft neckline, mid-calf hem and shoes, which were in another cupboard and recalled as dark brown and low-heeled. Patty slid back the doors with relish. The rails chattered quite companionably enough as she whisked out the items. A fresh scent of modern wardrobe came with them, knowing nothing of this past of sensible lecturer and mother she was to celebrate in this reunion.

'Tess will probably wear blue.'

'What?'

'Oh, I was thinking of Tess Thomas. She was Secretary for all those years. I've always had a Christmas card from her. She'll be there.'

'There'll be some husbands and wives as hangers-on, I suppose. We'll have to plan ahead.'

'I'll check on some Hotels in the region and take a one-nighter for us.' Patty's assumptions were nodded to as a go-ahead by Tim.

'Will Simon be there, do you think?'

'Almost bound to be, although I didn't hear from him at Christmas. He would let us know if there was an issue. The year before he put in a photo of his granddaughter.'

'They'll be coming from all over the place.'

'True,' said Patty.

When she had booked the small hotel in Cumbria for the night before the funeral date, Patty felt relieved on behalf of Lillian.

'She was so resourceful, Tim. Lillian looked ahead as much as a visionary might.'

'We're going to a funeral, not the Pearly Gates.'

Ulverston looked conspicuously underdeveloped as they drove the winding roads to the town. Lillian had retired to a peninsula and had been there for many years. She had been very proud of the area from her arrival. She pressed flowers as a hobby, particularly those wild flowers which grew between sea and shore, grasses and Plantain leaves and a purple, spiky flower like Michaelmas Daisy, but it wasn't, Patty knew. What a productive person Lillian was to find the time for notecard making, the sending of them, her comment on the flowers being enough to show that she was alert and active.

'I expect she was in all the local activities.'

'I've got no doubt she was.' Tim had drawn up at a crossroads.

'This is where I get my bearings.'

The late afternoon sunlight eventually lighted up the distant view of Furness Abbey and gave Patty the spur she needed. It had been a long drive despite Tim's well-timed breaks. She wanted to take as much stock of the area as she could. It was obviously in need of regeneration, but the sea refreshed in its own right.

'We're here, Patty.' Tim was a lot more focussed.

Patty wanted to keep her nose in the breeze, but Tim led the way up the Hotel steps from its car park in his very determined fashion. She knew he would find a golfer before or after their evening meal.

No Hotel stay of theirs unrolled quite like this one. At every sip of the opener wine she glanced round in case one of her former colleagues had booked in here too. An alphabetical list of addresses was unlocking in her head and even post-codes flashed by. Bennett, Sy, Simon, Head of Economics. He'd be here. His subject fitted Lillian like a glove. His youthful just-out-of-College smile reassured you that there was a human face to number crunching. Mildmay, Joyce. How she had blanched when cutbacks were announced. She juggled four kids and a husband in remission. Did all this blow in on the very air of the place to which they had all converged, knowing Lillian?

'I did find him, Patty.'

'What?'

'I just knew I'd find one.' Tim flexed his trouser knees as he sat beside her in the lounge. 'He's got exactly my handicap.'

'Oh.'

Patty lifted a brochure on the area from the rack of them nearby. Glossy photographs of the Abbey, evidently a very unusual one, the coast walk and the industrial heritage caught her eye in the all-too-bright colouring of such things. Lillian would have been active in all this. She was an amenity-conscious person, a social conscience on two strong legs. She was a pillar.

Next morning Patty took her outfit from the wardrobe and placed it across the roughly folded pure white of Hotel sheets. It looked bland, without any statement on its background there. She went to get her tights.

'We'll leave tonight shall we?' Tim was eyeing up the weather outside. 'It's better than when we arrived.'

Good travelling weather for the others on this September day. Patty thought through some opening sentences of renewed acquaintance, exploring ways to keep a conversation going. She thought of faces too.

'I'll know them by the shape of the head. That doesn't change, I do know,' she nodded to Tim across a quite wide breakfast table.

'Can you be sure you were being that observant in the first place?' Tim was in a talkative mood. He must be quiet for the funeral.

'Of course, Tim. Some I knew for years. They'd have weathered as well as I have.' She smiled as though feeling it must be the last for the time being. The funeral was in the next hour.

They walked up, slowed because of the newness of the small town streets, but deliberately because of the purpose for which they had come. Probably their gait was like everyone else's, with a formal knowingness and inevitability in each stride, a beat of memory you had hoped not to measure too soon or not now. Sy would be doing the same. She would hear about Joyce's children, aged about the same as their two, long flown the nest.

The tucked-away Church was a red-brick build of a recent, not Victorian past. Inside there was more light than you might have anticipated and it was a broad space, too, making it easy to see who was there. To quiet organ music they chose a mid-aisle row and shuffled along the range of pastel-padded wooden chairs to a centre position which suited them both. Tim took to the Funeral Service booklet as if he was looking for his Maker's name. He never did like hymns, Patty thought, if thoughts are what you have at funerals. Her mind was on the seats already filled, but the backs of heads did not give her the shapes she had mentioned to Tim so glibly. She always sized up her former colleagues from the front. She could not turn around and she would not.

The large, open space filled up. Then the well-dressed entourage processed in with Lillian's coffin ahead of their seats to place it prominently but low down. One wreath of flowers raised it just enough for it to be noticeable but not conspicuous.

Lillian's face looked out from the service sheet. The relatives had chosen a picture of her as Principal when she had medium length crisp, salt and pepper hair framing her face with its firm jaw. That pearl necklace hardly seemed to leave her throat and there it was again, centred beautifully, as if she never leaned forward to angrily confront anyone. She ruled with a confident will and now she lay silent just as everyone must.

When the coffin was taken solemnly to the waiting cars for the family's journey to its committal, organ music held people to their seats in respect, then there was rising, the turning, the moment Patty had anticipated for so long.

What greeted them both as they turned was a small troupe of young twenty-somethings in black dresses and white aprons, lifting lightweight tables down the aisle. A few young men in dark suits were intent on a well-planned tactic of stacking the chairs from which the congregation had just eased itself. Instead of the organ music, a homely buzz of voices, greetings and introductions filled the Church. In no time food was on the tables, waitresses were milling with plates of sandwiches and a large hatch was opened on the Church kitchen at the back for teas and coffees.

The slickness threw Patty and Tim together in a way they hadn't planned. Conspiratorially, over a cup of coffee each, the two of them measured up these convivialities which could not include them.

'What about that chap there?' Tim was being helpfully observant.

'Nothing like anyone I'm looking for.'

'That woman with the silver hair and grey jacket?' Tim indicated with a move of his coffee cup after a full swig.

'No, not a chance.'

This liveliness in death defeated Patty. Tim watched her eyes glaze. The two of them stood close together in their pincer movements of cup and saucer and other people's elbows.

Behind his wife's eyes, only recently brightened by the pearls recalled on Lillian's photograph, was a dulled truth. Time doesn't trade in deals of any kind.

'We'll have to go, Tim.'

There was no Lillian. There was no-one.

Cut to Inspire

'Quarter to nine already,' Gus said to himself.

A slight, oblique frame moved to the left as he walked with his two sticks. The right leg was skewed out at the knee to such an extent that weight bearing and balance could only be achieved with a stick for support. There was another for the left to adjust and to compensate for propulsion.

Gus was moving down an alleyway to the back of a short spread of mid-nineteenth shops in the centre of Salisbury. It was not a bustling parade. That just-before-nine-o'clock quiet had descended and it followed Gus deliberately around into the stillness of the backyard. The broadened space and its bins lent an air of scrupulous modernity to the scarred wooden shutters and back doors. Years before a yard, gardens or stables would have been there, with picket fencing cordoning off dwellings above the shops and space for children and washing.

Gus could tap by without restriction and came to the second door. He stopped his sticks, leaned forward to balance, got out the key and unlocked the door to his premises. His Barber's business had been going for just over a year. The lights came on in a flash at the back and front room together and they twinkled over four mirrors and basins ready for business. Jude would arrive at nine and Gus left the back door unlocked for him as usual. On Market Days, Gemma would let herself in.

The back room was as neat as a crew cut. Bespoke cupboards housed their products. A painted gate-leg table held the laptop, a vase of flowers and the occasional mug. Tucked in at the side was a granite-topped sink unit for domestic use. Coffees and croissants, paninis and sandwiches were available in the shops nearby. Gus's first outlay and resource plan was to promote a tell-it-as-it-is package of originality along with the basics of scrupulous hygiene. He never regretted working hard when he had set up the business. As always he hung up his sticks beside the back door to put on a butcher's apron of red stripes. There was a full drawer of these to be changed daily over the black shirts and trousers he required his staff to wear. Gus had come up with the idea of the outfit. Red and white striped apron, the Barber's pole, but black beneath instead of white as a Butcher would have. Barbers were surgeons no longer but sleek deliverers of a suave service.

Jude arrived as Gus opened the laptop, hands still a little stiff after the short walk from the car parked just off the narrow street.

'Mornin', mate,' was always Jude's way, whatever the weather. He had a day off midweek, so was fresh either side. Gus, the owner, worked the six days, nine till five. Picking up Jude had been a stroke of good fortune. He'd been straight out of a south coast College course only weeks before they met. They stood together in the back room, nothing doing until 9.30am, with time to fetch a coffee if they felt like it.

'Hi,' was the response. 'We're full today, so I'll need a cappuccino to start up. What are you going for?'

'To see Fran, of course,' Jude said as he went quickly off, a tall man and a counter to Gus's stoop.

Gus passed through into his shop. To enlarge its perspective, a near wall-sized mirror hung on the widest wall. It sat elegantly on a zebra-striped wall covering, clean-cut and exact for customers to view themselves, then see the end result.

Gus took his two sticks from a rack near the first sink, his shop floor pair, made of lightweight aluminium and as cleverly designed as a set of fencing foils. He took himself to each of the four sinks and mirrors to display fresh towels readied for the day. Each time, in order to use both hands, his sticks were hooked to one side of his butcher's pocket. Looked at in the mirrors over the wash basins they were like pairs of scissors, handles uppermost.

The day began with Walter, nicknamed 'The Walrus'. He came every fourth Monday, booking ahead like clockwork.

'Without you boys, I'd be done,' meaning his grisly looks would frighten the ladies.

'I was real dapper, once. Can you imagine me black as those zebra stripes of yours?'

'Yes and no,' Gus honestly replied as his eyes met Walter's in the mirror over the sink. A frizzle of hard, grey hairs edged his scissors.

'Lasted until I was about forty-five. You've still got plenty of time to go.'

The majority of customers were twenty-five and younger with cuts perched on necks of all lengths and widths. Gus and Jude knew how to weigh the head on the neck at the first look in the mirror. These guys didn't want tidy up, but needed style.

Josh was one who seemed to have more money than most. He picked a colour change every other month.

'Mood man, me, man,' was his mantra as though he painted the air around him with a brush of the day's colour. Today it was a pale blue stripe he wanted, from left ear over to the top of the skull to diffuse into a tuft of dark ginger.

Gus was expert at brush work. Silently and patiently he placed silver foil folds along the pleat that was wanted. Ginger dye first, dry it off, pat the hairline and carefully comb in and comb out the mid-blue and grey to produce the effect. To steady himself he would hold the back of Josh's chair, hung with a stark black towel, his choice of Barber's trademark. Otherwise, he leant only slightly. The sitting customer suited his stoop, keeping still so that only Gus's actions mattered. At these points of the procedure, customers bowed their heads and did not see the deft moves of the disabled barber, his knees bent at the swivel chair to balance, the body swaying at each snip and the splicing of hairs, tufts, layers and spacing, side to side.

'My mates need to see you doing this,' Josh said firmly. 'They think I'm a freak show until they see what you've done.'

'They could try it here, maybe? Get the feel of it, like you do?'

'They ain't got the money, mate. Some girl's taking it from all of them. Once that happens, they don't look after themselves.'

'Well, they'd do it a different way.'

'Yeah. Plain and ordinary, like.' Josh seemed sure of his ground.

'They go to 'Jack's' do they?' Gus felt he had to say.

'Wherever. There's a few in Salisbury. You'd know them all, wouldn't you?'

Gus certainly did. His first plan had been to join the opposition and not beat them. He'd researched Salisbury's road pattern and its critical Night Club area before he put any business plan together. His sturdier road sticks clicked on the pavements as he walked the route of his imaginary punters. The Cathedral even gave him his business name, 'Cut to Inspire'. As the customers left his neat Barber's shop, they saw its famous silhouette at the very end of the road.

Josh was a reliable customer. His choices were fastidious. Others were more certain of a classic cut and just a few didn't seem to mind at all. They came in on Market Days.

'How do you manage, mate?' always came first, then, 'Short back and sides,' as if the frontal lobe quiff was uniquely theirs to toy with in the mirror at home.

Alec looked at Gus one day, determined to live up to his proverbial name.

'From your vantage point, you're seeing a lot more of me than I'm seeing of you.'

'To do our job we need all round vision. You've got a hand mirror to see what I've done. We get the 3D view.'

Gus held the back of the chair firmly as he stopped to talk. Jude was working on a pal of Alec's in the opposite chair. He could see Jude's youthful face in the mirror, straight-faced, like they tell you in training, only ready to laugh when the shop was empty. You gave no clue when there was live flesh right beside you, paying you for your joke on them.

'What was he going on about?' said Jude when the two had left the shop. He had begun to sweep up, which Gus could not do so well. He would hoover, once weekly, with an adapted appliance.

'Not sure. I suppose they thought they could talk over our heads between the two mirrors as we had him and his pal both on the go together. Pity we can't do the same sometimes.'

'Do we listen, Gus? I'm not interested one bit.'

'Maybe, but most of our customers don't talk much.' Gus went through to the laptop. 'Come and see my revised database,' he called as Jude was making his way to the bin. He had also gathered up a few used towels.

'Look at these,' he said as he scrolled down the customer names. 'They might talk about Football teams, sometimes; girlfriends, never. Family, forget it, weather, boring. Clubs, well, you know what the punters'll say. As long as they've got money in the back pocket, I don't mind what comes out of their mouths.'

'I would, if I was you,' said Jude, unexpectedly. 'You're the boss and there's a few come in off the street who don't think so. I can see it on their faces.'

Gus was in charge of his back room sticks after leaning on the table.

'Oh, these, you mean? We've done all that chat, you and me. I did it all when I began the business. No change in all this, but plenty in the shop.'

'You're free next. I'll whip out and get you a coffee, okay?'

'Yes, thanks.'

At times like this, Gus knew why he had chosen this career path. He was on his feet all day, with even the speedy customer trapped, the challenge different every time. His job was based on what he could do with his hands, not on the stamina through his feet. He knew how he and his sticks on the move resembled a crab on dry sand, ungainly, keen to get somewhere safe. Here, on the Barber Shop floor, Gus was in his own safe rock pool. All the reflections on the water came from the sitting customers who could get up and walk away, leaving him and his safe pool behind.

He was able to observe, far more than his customers, the kaleidoscope of vanities which brought them to him. His job was to send them out with their pride massaged just a little. After all, the hair, what there was of it, was theirs and not his.

Not many months later, a Fair in the centre of the City had put all the local businesses into a flat spin.

'We'll cope, we'll cope somehow,' the numerous emails seemed hesitantly to expect. Gus got a friend of Gemma's to come by, to get used to their ways and to man the fourth basin for the week, just in case. Things went well for them until day four, a Thursday, when umpteen coaches had unloaded from other parts of Wiltshire and beyond.

Raymond looked as if he had come in to escape the crush in the town centre, but this Barber's shop had been manned to cope. He got given the girl for the week, Hayley.

'Can't abide these crowds. I get brought along to carry the bloody bags.'

His eyes had been on Gus all of the short time he had been waiting on the chairs provided. When he was in front of the mirror he became confidential. Hayley obligingly bent an ear to catch what he said to her.

'Is that the best this place can do?' In the mirror, Hayley saw him look pointedly at Gus who was working opposite. He had just walked back to his cutting position using his crutches and was hooking them on his apron pocket so as to continue with his customer.

'That's our boss,' was the best young Hayley could do in reply.

'You mean he thinks he is.' Raymond curled a middle-aged top lip as he nodded to Hayley to begin. 'I can't see a future for someone like him.'

Hayley looked at the man's face squared up in the mirror in front of her.

'I haven't known him long, but he's all right. He's good,' was what she managed to say before the mirror showed her the look of long-suffering on her customer's face and she was forced to begin. As she cut and trimmed, the room emptied. It was coming up to lunchtime.

'Daddy!' came a call as the shop door opened and a boy aged about three was let in by his mother.

'Gus, we're safe in here. I know we're not meant to disturb you in business hours but it's pandemonium outside. You'd never believe the crowds.'

'They can stay where they are. I've got you, love. Come through to the back. Just for family, I can shut for half an hour.'

Gus's young son ran through. Gus turned to Hayley.

'Get yourself some lunch when you've washed. I'll see to this gentleman. Just a bit more to comb through and he'll be ready for the fray. All right, sir?'

Raymond paid in silence.

'Thank you. Hope you find some space to stroll round the town.'

Raymond wanted to voice a considered opinion on parting.

'I was thinking this job would hardly suit someone like you.'

'Oh, it suits me fine. I can look at myself all day long.'

The Garden grows

The shadow of the window frame lay on the breakfast room wall, muting the cream, adding a cappucino froth to the plaster beneath.

Fenella watched the dark crosses of the frame move along the wall towards her as she gazed out on her garden. Her small garden demanded only one eye on its size if the other could watch the shadow on the wall. Two perpectives pleased.

It was a small terraced house which she owned, widowed into it and wedded to it now that only friends called. Family was too far-flung for her and, anyway, the grandchildren flounced. That would not do in her garden.

Fenella's plans grew with every tread of hers beyond the back door. That was the reason why she often stood at her window to look, expressing hope in the air above the garden, then firmly planting an idea with every footstep.

Fred came to visit just when the first of the vistas took place in her mind. Fred had been her husband's workmate.

'He'd have loved you all the more if he could see you now, Fenella. Look at what you've been able to do with the view.'

'Oh, that. It's not the best season for viewing, Fred, but my planning's in my head. I'm thinking of widening it out with very specialised planting. Do you have any tips?'

This something on her mind engaged Fred in a way she hadn't anticipated. It all relied on the light from the window.

'Colour's what you want to concentrate on, don't you think, Fenella? How about greys, greens and whites to keep the lightness you're aiming for?'

'Oh, I'm not looking for lightness, Fred. I want the darkness in too, to take you forward into the garden, secretive-like.'

Fenella knew she sounded like a Victorian madam with a bevy of men ready for the garden experience. A picture, was it Toulouse-Lautrec, entered her mind and exited in haste as Fred got up. He got up to look out of the window.

'It's not ready yet, Fred.'

'Oh, I get you, Fenella. Perfection only is it? I'll leave you to your pruning, if you like.'

'I don't mean you to go right away, Fred. Can I offer you some tea?' Fenella was moving to the kitchen.

'No, it's fine. I'll come by in a fortnight, as usual.'

In that two weeks of flowering time, Fenella had some opportunities to shop for the colours she knew would frame her widened garden.

The first was to get Marilyn, her neighbour, to join her for a pots afternoon.

'I can't see how you are going to find them, let alone fit them in. I can't abide clutter.'

Fenella was thankful that the wall on Marilyn's side had been raised with trellis long before she had bought the house. It was a pock-marked brick wall, screaming late Victorian. Curved bricks layered along the top, dipping and undulating where mortar was replaced by moss.

'What do you mean, they've got to be bright red?' Marilyn was ready to squabble about a statement of intent. How would a garden be that? Hers was a place to put the pot plants she was given on birthdays.

'Oh, you'll see soon enough. I'm trying to get the garden bigger, Marilyn.'

'You won't let anything trail over the wall, will you? You know how fast creeper can spread.'

Fenella's second plan was to be a coffee morning with Marilyn and her older sister, Zena, one day in early April.

The two ladies came in similar tops, but each a different colour. Zena wore blue and Marilyn yellow. They stood at the breakfast room window, eyeing the garden with doubtful looks as if they were pot plants themselves and glad of a consistent temperature.

'Coffee outside?' said Fenella, who had got the tray ready well before the early advance of a bluebell and daffodil into her garden.

Out of sight, around the corner of the L-shaped house, there was a small metal table, trellised in an eastern pattern, just right for crumbs to fall through the fretwork. It lived against the house wall and the neighbour's brick-work and, as a tidy representation of abundance, it held a potted plant.

'Just this corner, then? I see it's three chairs ready, but you could stretch to four.' Marilyn was pulling out one of the chairs as she spoke and each of the ladies took their places to face the width of the garden.

'This has got an airy feel,' said Zena, comfortably settled.

'You can't expect too much from a garden at this time of year,' said Marilyn, consoled by good coffee and its milky froth on top.

'I'll be in control of it by spring,' remarked Fenella as she picked up the biscuit plate. 'If this space above my head could feed down the garden, that would work for me, wouldn't it?'

'You make it sound as if you're planting on a trampoline.'

'Oh, anything up in the air will do,' was Fenella's reply.

As the two women left her garden, Zena looked back at it rather fondly. 'I think you're getting there,' she said.

A week or so later, Fenella was able to consider these words more carefully. Each perspective adds to a view and this was no exception. What would Zena make of the new path, the zig-zag to Marilyn's side with a sharp bend leading to the pond? It had been cut through scything grass, it seemed, and to peer down into the pond was to jump from a great height, if you were a caterpillar of the hairy variety, hairpin-bending its body up a stem of grass to produce a madam's hairstyle before the fall.

In early June she had five guests, making a half dozen for lunch in the garden. The gate-leg table in the kitchen came to life like a dog raising its leg on her pots, which were red and upright on a woven wigwam over to the bottom end, right. Fenella's eyes rested on the juicy plumpness of the early flowering on them. It was a fake fruitfulness down there, far away in the foliage and peeping reassuringly at her guests.

'You got us all in.' Jake said, as Fenella was the last to seat herself at the three-a-side table. The stools were sturdy and were stackable, but she had no need to explain as her guests covered them with flannel trousers, pleated skirts and cropped jeans to make a neat edging of lobelia blue as if they had planned it all. Of course, she had arranged a half dozen voices to speak in her garden, to garner what they could from her spacious plot. Gill hardly stopped talking over the quiche and salad.

'You'd have to go a long way to get this experience, Fenella. I don't think that I could have a lunch for six on my lawn. I can see you've got so much on the go down the end there. Have you put in the pergola? Clever you.'

Fenella served her guests. Elbow room was tight but not a problem to anyone. Fred was unusually complimentary.

'I haven't had a quiche like this for years, Fenella. You'll soon be growing the onions and keeping hens and pigs.'

His expansiveness cheered her on to the meringue nests with raspberries. In her mind she carried fulsome images of the tight corners she had enlarged, shaving off mosses and lichen, chasing worms into the soil beneath her twisting treasures, the creepers of every sort of green.

The breakfast room window began to ache with the heat of July days. The winding paths extended to a fine summerhouse. All the foliage of a hot day waved over Fenella as she passed it on a walk, then made her way to the 'long lake' and stood at its edge to look back at the house. Far in the distance, a small breakfast room window winked at her. Its frame was brightly whitened. The shadows had broken away.

This vista was what she wanted for her next guests, the Golf Club wives. She had not been in attendance at the Club for a number of years, but now was the time for re-acquaintance with the women of the green.

Anticipating twenty, Fenella hired in three long trestle tables with stacking stools. Cartwright's came up with a catering plan and with plates and cutlery made to look as real as if they needed washing up. Even black bags were provided and a two-girl team set it up for 2pm.

One of the girls, Bligh, moved with speedy efficiency. Jaycee brought the food.

'It's a spread you look as if you deserve in a garden like this one,' said Bligh, and raised a head from her tasks. 'There's more than enough room for all the ladies.'

'Have they seen it before?' said Jaycee, with her hands full of cutlery wrapped in cream napkins. 'You'll definitely surprise them if they haven't.'

Even that non-committal conversation spurred Fenella on. She wandered down to adjust a fern and pulled at a stray twig of topiary peacock.

'They'll love your food,' was what she said.

The grand outdoor meal was so successful that every guest wanted to come again and said so many times.

'Who wouldn't eat out in a garden like this?'

'Good feel in the air, Fenella. It's wonderfully arching over us this garden of yours, and all without shade. How do you manage it?'

No reply was expected as Fenella was kissed by all on the way out. The breakfast room and hallway bulged with summer dresses and the sound of that special care taken with the tread of sandals and open shoes. Fenella turned back from each of the farewells to a garden full of roses.

A phone message had come through whilst the guests were there. There was to be a family visit towards the end of the school holidays. Catherine, who lived in the Midlands, was to stop by on the way to the Channel Tunnel and the family would be round for an afternoon coffee.

'We understand you're so cramped.' Catherine's message said. 'Phoebe and Rory will be all right with it.'

'I know,' replied Fenella, when she rang back to confirm.

It was a half-bright day when the family arrived. Catherine's husband drove off to fill up with petrol, and daughter gave a welcoming hug accompanied by, 'Hello, Granny,' from the two children. They had miles to go. The breakfast room shot bright and dark in an instant as the clouds played footie with the sun and at one intense burst, Phoebe and Rory jumped up from the carpet to stand by the window.

'Can we go out into the garden? It looks as if we could run down to the lake.' Phoebe's feet were moving on the spot as she spoke. Fenella stood up with a mug of coffee in her hands.

'Oh, yes, of course you can, but there's a wall. There isn't any further, Phoebe dear.'

Hugh goes aloft

Hugh Andrewes was going to attempt to explode his wife's mythology. She had left him with her head full of ideas about Cathedrals, of all places.

'They rise above us, Hugh,' she told him in a reflective tone, 'and they can tell you a lot.' Olivia had said she'd visit a few Cathedrals on his behalf, so Hugh made a contrary plan to visit them himself as a circular tour of the spirit. His spirits always needed keeping up.

He set off at once to Winchester, from one capital city to the older one. He had a decent enough trip to it.

'Tell us a lot of old rot,' was what he had thought, but now it was time to enter the first Cathedral of the three, to please Olivia.

Hugh went through the opened door with a party of tourists and let them go ahead of him as he looked up. He was tall, thin, greying and undistinguished in their small crowd.

'Longest nave,' was clear.

Hugh was argumentative right at the start.

'But doesn't a roof have a longest, too?'

'A Moses basket upside, down,' he thought, and was reminded of a colouring exercise at school as he looked up. The roof resembled the buttoning on a vast leather sofa, for reclining cherubs and other cronies of the Almighty.

'What in heaven is happening up there? This is a ship of fools all right.'

Hugh, engineer, was used to asking questions for remedial answers. That roof was asking no questions, it was only providing answers to what he thought were geometrical questions.

'The marble font is stood on a stone base.' The guide spoke smoothly with an unprovocative tilt of language, but Hugh had queries of his own.

'I want to know if that tub was cast or carved?' he thought as its blackness stood out in relief like tooled pewter in front of him. 'Oh well, I won't cry at no answer. I'm sure there have been enough tears round here from wetted babies bawling their heads off.'

He remembered childless Olivia and was proud he had.

As the group moved on up the long aisle, Hugh heard a few key words and phrases. 'Originally Norman, Perpendicular, ribbed,' and his training kicked in.

'All this is excess.'

He stuttered his 's' sounds like a hiss.

'No wonder the ship is sinking under its own weight.'

He thought of the water beneath this Cathedral, flooding the crypt like the Nile itself.

'This is Hampshire's Nile Delta around the time of a certain Pharaoh, who was cruel!' The story from the lesson had hit home. No river bank, no Moses. No Moses, no story.

The laced basket bobbed on through his colouring hand, out of sight into the reeds. The rushing water went out to sea to be recycled for the annual floods. Moses was recycled like that, a story to circle between earth and heaven, a watery heaven, Sheol.

Hugh followed, rather than led his flock, on down the long nave which was far too long for a wedding.

'Our Registry Office affair was quite good enough at the time and I wasn't going to let sentiment sway me either.'

Outside, where an earlier Cathedral ground plan sat starkly outlined on the grass, Hugh looked down at this Cathedral ghost, the lost earlier statement. It looked shrivelled and it had no voice.

Hugh turned and began to contemplate the next visit. He had meticulously planned so that travel and stays were no problem. The problem, rather, was Olivia. Would she appreciate what he was trying to do? He couldn't argue it through any more. His attempts at reformation surprised him just as did his entry into the Cathedral, unaccosted and free. He felt the new leeway being given to him.

At St. Albans, Hugh looked up and quickly looked down again as he followed a smaller tour group in.

'Wouldn't get far in an old boat like this,' he remarked to himself, as he'd seen the Roman bricks on the exterior before entering.

'This is early recycling and no mistake and I bet there are more than a few leaks. Even old Noah used a decent plan and a decent wood.' He almost nudged an elderly gentleman in the ribs as he voiced this to himself.

Hugh's eye caught all the oddities of curves and cantilever as he listened acutely to the diminutive guide, a lady with fading grey hair and a glow in her eyes which spoke of the youth she had lost.

'Our pride and glory,' she clippingly and clearly spoke, 'is the screen, now without its original statues.'

'This old dear is an original, I'm sure of that. Everyone a 'one-off' as they say. What's lost from the original doesn't make it less original. But, after all, a bit of de-cluttering doesn't do any harm.' He almost spoke to the slight figure who was absorbing his attention more than he felt she ought.

Then, it was beyond the screen to the Lady Chapel. The little lady launched.

'This is a truly wonderful addition, extending the length of the Cathedral, just at the time when these Chapels were becoming a symbol of national importance.'

'Too many pregnant words,' he almost retorted. 'I'm an engineer. The meaning is in the structure, not what we say the structure is.'

"Light falls where it will, in shafts th'Almighty knows'. I must be quoting a poem from school,' he thought and, unnervingly pitching into childhood's manners, suddenly found himself nodding obediently to a teacher. 'Always a lady teacher in those days,' he thought for the first time, 'and here am I 'being a good boy' for her. Olivia should have known me when I was younger. Pity we couldn't have been childhood sweethearts instead of marrying so late as we did.'

He looked up, then turned to follow again. Perhaps teacher was taking them to the lunch hall.

He'd planned a break of a couple of days before the trip to Ely and had a few thoughts on eels, mostly leading nowhere. Ghostly, mysterious creatures was all he could finally think.

At least the Cathedral at Ely didn't need to be approached. There was no wide green, no gate. It was there, lopsidedly central on the Isle, the town and road, which meandered very close to the West front.

'I'll get up if I can,' thought Hugh, nimbly ducking a tourist camera before stepping adroitly inside with the same small, clicking party. Cameras awry, they were pausing to look up at a tapestry of a painted ceiling stretching away above an abundant aisle of vast pillars. Arch upon arch caught the sun's shafts as if Giotto had painted before stone had ever been worked.

Above them he stared.

'Those Bible characters up there would smile if they realised the risk,' a slight ache in his neck was telling him, but the figures led onward exhorting the lessons of belief held by so many. He knew he'd coloured in a few characters at school and picked them out with glee.

'Old Abraham, look! When teacher told me how many sheep he had, I gave a little clap under my desk.'

Even now Hugh felt the dynamic of the story with all its threat and thrust. He found himself ahead of the flock, so decided to take a lead this time.

He was the first of the group to reach the eight-sided central tower and his eyes widened in disbelief as a star burst in front of them.

'This can't happen!' he almost yelled at his flock. More cautiously he gnawed at his thoughts instead.

'An engineering masterpiece. Impossible.'

He ran over to a model of the miraculous lantern tower, looking insignificantly scaled down on a table in the transept. He and his small group stood around it. There was no guide to explain. Miracles don't need explanation he thought, then he saw a fellow tourist pointing out the times for Octagon Tours. Ten minutes to wait.

Leaving his group at the start point, Hugh wandered back down the nave counting the massy pillars and looking at the painted roof from the other direction. Walking to the West, Hugh was aligning his wide stride to the distance between the stone sentinels. He was aware of numerous visitors coming in one by one through the small door into the West porch.

Back at the Octagon space, he sat down on one of the many chairs provided, cursing Olivia for her astuteness.

'They tell you things, Hugh,' her voice nagged him.

Stunned by the evidence that thin air held a roof as high up and proud as this one, Hugh remained seated, keeping an eye on his flock standing alongside the meaningless model. He seemed to soar into the great emptiness holding the heavenly roof above and was surprised at his light-headedness.

A middle-aged gentleman in a crew cut jumper with enough cable stitching to prove him a mariner, came to take the half dozen on the upward tour.

'Three levels.' Hugh paid enough attention to hear him say.

'The top isn't for the faint-hearted and all the doors on the way are very narrow, like the stairs.'

This punchy warning didn't seem to alarm the crew, as Hugh found himself calling them.

'We're going aloft,' he attempted to boom, but decided to concentrate on twisting stone stairs with rope handrails for those with a rolling gait.

Hugh ignored the time-honoured flow of the excellent guide, noting his calculated rests for the ladies and the not so young, just like himself.

Features and fittings viewed from an interior height were of no interest for Hugh, but at second level they were led outside into a gentle wind where buttresses did only a fraction of what that immense octagon could do.

Hugh was impatient to secure his engineer's heaven and give praise for the miracle which he would soon have under his hands.

They came at last to the interior corona and were left alone to circle the vast wood structure in front of them. The midget model in the transept now materialised in its true space.

Hugh's breath was drawn in so sharply, his ribs might almost have ached.

'There's no span. It's all balance, thrust and pressure! It's a nothing keeping heaven in one place.'

He saw the others opening the high doors of the painted cage, where larger than life-size angels primly and blushingly looked down onto the Cathedral's interior far below.

Hugh brushed along as many of the dozens of thick, black, wooden beams as he could, and smiled at their dark patina of mediaeval confidence.

'The ship's rigging is secure and it's been on a voyage for as many years as these trees are old.' He felt he knew about contemplation as he ended his tour on the open roof, feeling at one with these fellow sailors and the Captain.

'Learning by doing up here. No more colouring books, flat, one dimensional. I'm holding tight and I know I'm safe in 3D real,' he almost whistled, or thought he heard the bosun whistle to be down.

It was then he found himself in the very centre of the tiled floor labyrinth at the West door, just as his wife opened it to enter.

Widowed Olivia began where Hugh had ended. She looked right down the length of the nave so as to adjust to the space after stooping her slight frame through the narrow door.

'It's me, Olivia! I've done all the visits for you. Bet you're surprised to find me here!'

Olivia walked through his space, merely taking his former shadow with her as she paused with her handbag to take stock.

She went over to the Welcome desk eager to pay for consolation.

Lawn Matters

The first spade dissected her small rose bed. Right in the centre stood the boots of the man who had stepped over her Rosa rugosa as if it were a ten-a-penny tuft.

The second spade was wielded over the vegetable patch beyond the weeping silver birch. Through the faintly-forming green haze of the spring growth Clare saw a black spike pumping up and down.

It was a grey-suited man who first informed her.

'We've had instructions to dig up your garden. I'll be putting in the team at once. They know the drill.'

There was no-one to whom she could turn. The last two years had been very guarded ones. Clare dwelt in relative security. George was a golfer, Rotarian and an aspiring District Councillor who retired at only fifty to pursue this add-on career. Then, he'd gone.

'Bacon with that egg, George?' was her unforgettable final remark. She had assumed a 'yes' and went back to the kitchen to find the bacon, to put on more toast, to listen to the radio's shrill- voiced Government Minister and had returned. The empty room crackled at her overfull mind.

Of all subsequent days, full of angles on where George could have gone, this first day was the very worst. She had put the plate of steaming bacon down, toast rack alongside, turned off the radio and stood in the silence which she had already appreciated as irrevocable. The room itself told her so. She looked down at the empty chair where George had sat with the newspaper only five minutes before. She glanced at the clock. Time had not stood still after all. Routine and the unexpected together gave her no insulation. Goose bumps arrived, and she trembled as if to shake them off like talcum powder after a bath. She knew George had not gone upstairs. There was no tell-tale creak of a certain floorboard on which he always trod heavily if the bathroom called. The front door had not slammed. She went to look.

It was open to its fullest extent as though an army might enter or evening guests arrive far too early for comfort, one after the other in disconcerting consort.

'George,' she had called. He might have followed the postman for a signature on a parcel, or have been caught by Emily from two doors down. She always set off with her dog at about this time.

There was no-one on the pavements of their cul-de-sac, no car in their drive. Over the nagging, repetitive words of a Cabinet minister, George had driven off with no explanation and no goodbye.

Later, she wished for every ounce of the concentrated quiet gained in those first moments of mild panic. She waited, of course, as any wife would, expecting an answer to this inexplicable taking off on his own. Was it something George had suddenly remembered, a text in the night hours, a niece's birthday present? His mobile phone was in the usual place. He had left without a coat and in that coat she had found it with the clean handkerchief and the comb. What clueless items these? What April aberration had turned his mind on this Spring day?

'Do you know of any reason why he should leave? We need to ask you as many questions as will jog your memory. What was his memory like?'

As the Missing Persons Enquiry entered a third week, April had become a wilful May. Blossom blew across from neighbouring gardens, flossing the pavements with recalcitrant petals. They were teased into corners to curve them with a short-lived pastel beauty. Then showers shocked them into a miserable brown curd, to be cuffed by the back legs of dogs and picked over by blackbirds until Spring was tired and disintegrated.

'I'm keeping up a routine as best I can, Jim.' This reply to the sum of concern expressed by the Local Council representative with one less at his Committee meetings.

'Your Dad wouldn't have left unless it was for a very good reason. We simply don't know what it is yet.' This to be helpful to Christopher, their son, on his Gap year in Australia.

'I'm answering all their questions and there's a good few I'm asking myself, and no mistake.' This to Carrie, her friend of thirty years. 'It's as if I never knew him. I'm beginning to sound like a cheap novel.'

'Not a bit of it. This is shock, just shock and anxiety, Clare. You're hardly yourself with this on your mind.'

'You'd have thought they could have found him in all this long summer.'

'It's not simply opportunity, though, is it? It's resources.'

'They tell me about manpower, you know. Truth is, there's no motive we can make out, so it all hangs on sightings, CCTV and that sort of thing. How can he be somewhere and yet not moving? George took himself off to do we don't know what we don't know where. It'll soon be six months. Christopher's coming back home in October to start Uni. George'd want to be around then. I just can't think how he could contemplate doing this to us.'

It wasn't the first time Carrie had listened to the same outpouring. Her problems were nothing like as serious. It was usually car keys. The longest search had been only half an hour. Even so, recriminations were like body blows.

'If you knew where you last had them, then we'd find them in seconds, but you don't know, do you?'

Unlike car keys, there are places too numerous to mislay a husband. Clare was forced to place the unseen George in a framework. His interests, driving routes, hobbies, shopping patterns, anything done on his own considered as if she was a drone observing his every individual circumstance. Each possibility was stifling, uncomfortably imagined and probably very far from the truth, if the truth were known.

This is what George'd had done. He had thrown her into a myriad of lies and conjecture. These pleased the consoling Policewoman who visited weekly in the first year. Together they got down to websites and Helplines. Helping was this woman's training but sympathy has so hard an edge at times like these.

'I wouldn't like to be in your position, but a good many people are. Exchanging information can't be a bad thing. It's keeping all the avenues open.' The textbook phrasing took away Clare's personality at a stroke. Clare had mislaid the other half of her life. It was like being given a broken oar to spin her round into unwelcome possibilities which took away any stability she could gain even from damned annoyance.

She was desperately annoyed with herself, with everybody. She couldn't propel herself into calmness however hard she tried.

No spades were in evidence when Christopher did pitch up, much more like a long-lost son than Clare had ever anticipated.

'Your beard looks better in the flesh than in the photographs.' She used a tone of nonchalance rather than the guilt she felt wanting to keep him at home when he'd freed himself as sons and daughters are meant to do.

'What've you been doing to cure the waiting?'

'Oh, some positive things. I'm at the Gym. I'm still on that Charity Committee and I'm endlessly at coffee with anyone who'll have me.'

'Good,' was the best Christopher could do before going off to Newcastle. He was to have a term or two there to settle in before the decision was made to investigate their garden.

Clare hadn't been in the mood to keep the garden up over the seasons since that egg and bacon for breakfast had all but ended her serious life. Some of the lawn she had finely mown, mostly right close to the conservatory and over to the small pond where their alfresco dining took place and the gazebo was. Beyond, round the otherwise quite happy rose beds, there was a wilderness style of down-trodden grass over to the vegetable plot.

'My garden's got rough, of course it has,' she tried to explain to faithful Carrie. 'But who would have expected this?'

'Treat it as a positive. Start all over when they've gone.'

'They won't find anything, unless the previous owners put Granny down.'

And so she watched from the kitchen window. Drainer on the left, dirty mugs on the right, movement like a comfortably ticking clock and accurate, too, these tasks at the sink.

Another grey-clad operative made his way to the vegetable patch this morning. A silent film began between her kitchen window curtains with Pathe-Pictorial opening music.

'We know we'll find the body, Madam.'

'You killed your husband for his money.'

'This is no ordinary rose bed.'

'How could you think such things?'

The comic scene worked and she turned away with a smile to take her coffee cup to a windowless seat.

They found nothing, and were their faces red? Not a bit of it. Her green lawn settled down into the edged lines of turfing laid with pile-driving thumps over a whole week in late October. Delays had been down to costs was the explanation, and she was given a quarterly update from the Missing Persons Enquiry reserve team.

'How many people do you never find? How many people like me have life on hold like a mystery drama on pause button?'

She wasn't frantic now, three years on. Christopher was thriving on no interference, so George really had blurred the edges after all.

'I think I've forgotten what missing is,' she said to Carrie, her litmus paper still for her thoughts on George.

'You'll have Christopher here for Christmas, like last year?'

'Christopher plus one. There's a girl friend staying for a few days.'

'Nice one, Clare. That'll keep you busy.'

Of course it did, but not enough to make the New Year an opener of any cheer. Holiday plans were on hold, just like the previous three years. Clare didn't visit George's family members as everything had been said that could be said about the resilience needed for the emptiness in her life. She might put up a sign, rakishly askew, in her front window, as a Boarding House landlady. 'Husband gone - Position Vacant'. There were a number of empty rooms.

It was a blustery style of March when the deadpan voice of her link at the Enquiry Service showed her how numbed she had become. Reaction didn't seem at all appropriate as she heard this proffered information.

'Mrs. Taylor, a man has been found matching the description of your husband, George, and we'd like you to come over to meet him.'

'Meet him, where?' Clare was pleased with her response.

'Come to the Central Bureau first. You know where we are. Then we'll move on.'

Clare knew the route to the Police HQ very well. This was not a quarterly meeting, but she had to make it seem it was. Hopes could not be raised, not because they might be dashed, but that hope had no face any more. It didn't even have George's face with an imagined sallow complexion after so long, or a tan from living the high life abroad. It needed to be a blank, so that she would know him as he was, if this man was George.

'We're very aware that it's been a long time, Mrs. Taylor. A gentleman has just been admitted to hospital in Doncaster with a touch of hypothermia.'

'My God, living rough?'

'That may be the case. We'd get you there within the hour. It's your decision.'

George was sitting up in the General Medical Ward, his shoulders resolute on the pillows behind him just as they had when he'd been down with 'Flu ten years before, but there was no smile for his wife, bringing tea to his bedroom. His face registered movement but not who was making it, so Clare walked up to him slowly, with the motions of any visitor moving to a bedside.

'George. It's me,' said Clare, and looked into clouding, doubting eyes before turning to the Ward Sister beside the curtains, ready to draw them and to leave them together.

'I'll have a word. How did he get here?'

'It's very likely that he's been looked after by some of the locals, living rough, but in and out of the hostels to get fed. This weather is unusually cold and your husband probably got caught out by it. The Street Pastors took him in.'

'What sort of recovery time are we looking at?'

'We've done some tests. His chest isn't weakened too much, but he's very unresponsive and unsure. When he's back on his feet we'll be able to assess how his dementia has progressed.'

Clare glanced at George. He was looking in their direction and not seeing either of the two women.

'It's unusually early for the onset of dementia. You haven't seen him for a while, then? Did he wander off?'

'Yes, he did. He just walked out. It's been four years.'

Stomping ground

'You just can't do that, Keira,' her mother shouted from the kitchen.

'Oh, yes I can and I will.'

Keira came into the kitchen as she replied, her frame boned and weighted to go ahead into trouble. Trouble was that her mother was tall, too, big-boned and well-dressed. She was made-up in the way she would have Keira kitted out when she got herself a job. The dream was vanishing. The girl had added defiance to definiteness and applied a liberal helping of odium to co-operation. It was fight and fighting talk from morning to night during the school holidays and torture every evening of term when school work had to be done.

Keira had begun to look upon her mother as a foreigner when she reached the age of twelve.

However hard she tried to be kind to the woman who had adopted her as a baby, the wrong words came out. It takes a very short time to be at war.

'We've done everything we could for you, Keira,' was a constant theme from her mother.

'So, I've got to live with that, have I? That you've done everything? You only think you've done everything and that the sums add up. We've got different totals, Mum.'

Kiera was practised at war. She remembered one of her birthday parties. It was her twelfth. The memory never faded for her because she had fancy-filmed it that day and filed it under 'Friends'.

The invitation cards were lavender-edged and spangled with silver stars. They were coveted by those who would receive one as Kiera's parties were always candyfloss affairs. If you got invited, you too were star-spangled for the following year.

'It'll all work out nicely,' she had said to the group given the invitations, 'I'm going to have cup cake muffins this year instead of a big cake. Mum says they'll look lovely on the stand, and I'll be having a lesson in how to make them, because they're off to a dinner party. When they come back they'll be surprised with what I've done. Then, we eat them at the party.' She waved her arms to her circle of friends. Her shining face and jerky movements kept them mesmerised.

They could not know that Keira's thoughts were like night without stars. As she turned round from her circle of friends, her years of birthdays seemed to rap on her knuckles one by one. Birthdays celebrated a bond which was never there. It was the child's only, not the mother's, and rap by rap each knuckle clicked more loudly and echoed more strongly each year the distancing between them.

Filling that widening space with friends and fun and laughter and something new was easy. Her parents had more than enough to give her. They lived in an area where a couple of TV stars also lived their private lives. It was countryside close enough to London for easy travel and its fields circled round a country town defending privacy by its downright drabness. With one of those celebrities living right next door, Keira's stardom was assured. She could be a head taller than the rest.

When her parents left for the dinner, Keira stood alone in the bright, white kitchen of her home with its soft lime-green walls above the tidy units. She moved a large, flowering white orchid out of the way on to a farther table. Like all the rooms in the house, the kitchen was a larger than average space, widened by whiteness and neatness. Mum wanted it to be an eternal Spring, but there were never any wild flowers, Keira thought.

She settled to the task. All the muffins baked earlier were cooling on a wire tray. The butter icing filled a large bowl which she took from the fridge and its colours and decorations were hers to command. Iced flowers, hundreds and thousands, violet flakes, silver sugar and jelly sweets of all colours were laid out for her. Her creations were to be far and away more definite than the flat-topped shop bought ones. Icing always pulled away on their silver, crinkly edges, just when you needed to be sweeter.

'Make twelve,' she thought. 'I'll be on TV as I create them, like Madge next door.'

'For our easy Cup Cake Lesson today, viewers, there's something individual for each of your guests,' she said with confidence.

How to make sense of this. She started to decorate for her friends. It soon began to go wrong. Alice's should be creamy with her red hair glowing, but Keira blobbed on the red first and its buttercream consistency resisted her palette knife to smooth it. The icing stood up in vibrant peaks to represent her fiery friend.

Next she hooked out a few glacé cherries from a small dish, stirred rather less red colouring into a small amount of buttercream and took the palette knife to spread and shape it. Simply swirled, it rose to a crown which she flattened with a cherry.

'That's for red nose,' she spoke out loud. There was no script now. 'And you'd improve with some silver sparkle. Let's powder your nose!'

Now lemon. Keira reached out for the pale shade, thinking viciously of little, frightened Emily. She towered over her in Netball games and she blamed her when the team lost.

'That's for you,' she said as she snaked down the side of the cascading lemon ice a helter-skelter ridge with the blunt knife. 'You're a jelly, so here's one for you,' and sneered as the sweet was placed on the spiral.

'Now for Jane and that stupid blue eye-shadow she wore at last year's party.' She coloured up a lighter blue shade, a sky blue ski mountain, pointed and pinched with white sugar flowers falling down it.

'You can do better, viewers, than Smarties on the top,' pouted Keira to her kitchen.

Pink follows blue, she thought, and created a flame pink fuzz, patting the knife tormentedly round the topping of flamingo cream. Her ballet dancing friend didn't need a cherry or a flower, but a crown. She tipped on the silver balls which slipped disobediently out of position.

'That'll serve her right.'

And so it went on. Each creation caricatured her forlorn friends until Keira had to complete the twelfth for herself.

She looked up with shock at the camera and shouted into the emptiness, loud enough for a recording studio to hear. Quite loud enough for mother and the star-studded friend next door to pay attention.

'You can't make me say what you want me to say!' she shouted.

She looked down at the other cup-cakes. They were like plugged-in lights twinkling garishly in the spot-lighted kitchen. There was no colour palette left for her except the opposite of white. Her black thoughts, so well fixed, she could not think at all. The mix in her TV show was all wrong. She was a rogue ingredient, spoiling the taste for the others because they had no taste for her. She decorated everyone's life but her own.

She picked up the final muffin, scooped out the centre with a spoon and placed in it a cherry for a heart. Piling creamy, zesty lemon icing on top, she put dobs of pink and blue around the sides, finally whirling them into a kaleidoscope which was topped with a white sugar flower.

She looked up to smile at the camera. The TV lights were certainly trained on her now.

'And that, viewers, is how it's done,' she proudly announced, putting down the knife.

'I'm leaving for Jake's as soon as term is over.'

Keira was in that same kitchen with the same mother who had served up so much of her life on a plate.

Fright, despair and disgust came over her mother's face.

'You'll be someone else's and you won't like it, Keira. Jake's not a good influence and his friends will be even worse.'

'That's what I want, Mum. Don't you understand after all these years? I'll be happy without the money, more than you think.'

'I've stopped thinking for you, Keira, and now I'm going to stop thinking of you. Your Dad will agree. We'll cut you right out of everything.'

'That's perfectly okay with me.'

Keira had met Jake at the end of one of her many taxi rides to and from Clubs in the town. She could easily look five years over age and make the most of it. Thick reddened lips gave her the look, and Jake, an import into this unenterprising market town, had come on the scene just after her sixteenth birthday the previous October. The opportunity not to be missed, to upset all the apple carts Keira had felt packed around her since childhood. She wanted those apples rolling. Calculated sleaze would be the new viewing.

Jake wasn't the first either, but this one would get back to Mum by the gossip channels and Keira would be more than glad. They were invited down to a squat in London, then with son, Benjy, Keira was set up in a small London flat, white walls packed with posters and door opened on certain visitors she knew how to test.

'We're not asking you to do anything that all the other Mums don't do. It's essential Benjy has his jabs in the right order.'

'You're not ordering me to do anything. I'm deciding in my own time.'

'But it's his time now, Keira. It's his right, not yours.'

'I don't want no cheek about rights. What rights have I had? Who let me have mine all those years of growing up?'

'Get out of your head you've been hard done by and get on with the job of this one. Benjy's lovely and anyone in your family would love him.'

'Oh, no, they wouldn't.' Keira winced and picked up Benjy from where he was lying on the play-mat. 'He's lovely for me. He's just what I wanted. Mum'll find him difficult to accept, like me. Me and Benjy'll get on very well together.'

On the Road

'I tell you it's an equitable drive! If you're using long words, Bella, then so can I.' Andrew's anger was directed to the road and not to his wife.

'I only meant keep over slightly. You're usually so good with Roxie.'

'You're off alignment, is good, coming from you!'

'So? If you can't keep Roxie centred, I'll take the reins.'

A couple of horse-lovers these, tamed by being too long together, disputing on a cosy ride along a country road. Quite straight this particular one, so that their cart could be seen by motorists from a distance. It carried on for a couple of miles for the practice purpose of their run.

'I'll be okay, Bella. It's the left of the axle I can hear. I must have been listening to that and veered slightly.'

'We'll soon be at the turn.' Bella kept things straightforward when there was a horse in earshot.

Beck's Farm gate was on the right at the conclusion of the outward ride that lunchtime. Swinging round and in, the Governess cart was as steady as the day she was made for an Edwardian brother and sister, somewhere in the Peak District, Andrew's research had informed him. That was what he was, a researcher, a perfectionist working in his double garage and shed, patiently piecing together the components of a lightweight cart.

'Okay, Bella, stay with Roxie, while I examine everything.'

Andrew gave the reins to his wife and got up. He opened the small retaining door in the rear where a metal step looking not unlike an overlarge serving slice enabled a governess and child or two to negotiate the height off the ground. It was a high vehicle with two tall, spoked wheels. Andrew's pride in the reconstruction of what had been a rusted wreck found in a local barn was reflected in the polished mahogany widely rimming the top of the cart. Like a fairground dodgem car it was padded and polished to give a comfortable ride over a bumpy surface. The wide wheels with such delicate spokes were made for this light cart to be shafted with a pensioned-off horse or a family pony, to ensure a safe, short journey.

'We've put it through its paces on that one then,' Andrew called up. He had been concerned about several spokes. Roxie would stand still while he inspected.

The handsome mustard-coloured chassis glowed in the dry farmyard entry. Andrew walked around the vehicle assessing it for parallels and curves, the mahogany of the mud guard, broad widths of steamed wood and steel with rubber springing, the trapezium of the rear door and those delicate spokes.

'What do you think?' came Bella's voice from above the tail of patient Roxie.

'It's good. It's good.'

Back to back in bed that night, Andrew was quieter than usual, Bella thought.

'Anything up, Andrew? It was a perfectly okay ride out today.'

'No, nothing up, but I'm not down.'

'Hmm. That's means you are.'

Andrew was considering the ride. 'Okay', rankled a bit. He felt he should have been riding on air with all the effort he had put into the cart in his spare moments over the last months. His shed held the hissing steamer used to soften the taut, thick leather of the cart springs. Its teasing sound had been singing in his ears since he lay down. How much more he could do to equilibrate the balance of the ride was debatable. No-one but he would know how this type of springing, the metre and a half's worth of leather and shot-steel arched together like giant eyelids half-open, taxed his ingenuity. His shed did the work of a smithy from the past and he a Farrier's odd-job man. He needed to feel the movement right on the road. Rather like the bed in which he was lying so comfortably with its sprung, balanced and unprovoked comfort, the ride ought to be as good as a salesman's description of ease, indisputable and practical.

'I'll give it a bit of thought,' Andrew murmured in reply.

'Oh, the cart, you mean?' Bella didn't think it could be anything else.

After that weekend, Andrew was in his car on the way to work. It was a village-to-village drive to a country house Research Unit. He was Chief Chemist and worked in one of the many outbuildings with a couple of staff who knew his ways well.

'How was your weekend?' Andrew spoke to Lucy, one of the Lab assistants.

'Really good, thanks. I decided on a drive out yesterday afternoon, not something I'd done for ages.'

'How far did you go?' Andrew had reached for a Lab coat.

'I surprised myself, rooting on for about forty miles. I went Coddenham way, you know, when you get off the A Road at Debenham.'

'I do, but what about the flooding that way? I've heard it's bad.'

'It's all over the place, Andrew. What a winter. It's March now and that February rain is still trying to find a way to drain.'

'It's fine down my way, of course. Long straight road, no dips or curves.' Andrew turned to get on.

It had been a very difficult winter in East Anglia. The driest part of the country had flooded wherever there was a river or the shadow of an old one. Nooks and crannies became running water courses of silvery widths or muddy strings. It surprised the locals when ditches filled up that had never carried much in living memory. These tales came from chats in the pub, the milkman on his rounds, and the early commuter caught out on his usual road and then on another route found to be just as impassable.

On his drive home that day, Andrew was testing how much of the chemist in him considered the make-up of the road surface. The springiness of the asphalt, the tension between heated chemicals, overused surfaces and saturated ground under the wheels of his old BMW, were all captured momentarily by a practical imagination.

'Doesn't seem to matter how they surface the road these days,' he remarked to Bella over a quickie pizza he'd agreed to that evening.

'Someone will have to think about it when these floods eventually go down.'

'It takes an age to get back to a level. We need a long, dry Spring.'

Bella reached over Andrew on the sofa.

'Look here.' The newspaper was opened with one hand. 'Biggest problem seems to be the road to the coast. Barton Hamlet is the only diversion and lorries are crumbling the country roads. I heard that they can't find a way to pump out the water, because it's an ancient mere that's appeared. The A Road goes right through. You couldn't make that up, could you?'

Andrew took the newspaper from Bella.

'Oh, I see. The surface water might drain down the hill, but it can't while the underground water keeps feeding it. It's a permanent paddling pool at the moment, evidently.'

Andrew got up with his plate, handing the local paper back to Bella. 'No knowing how long it will take.'

Bella got up, too. Andrew would be off out to his shed.

'I'll need you to take that road, though, Andrew, sometime in the next fortnight. It's the feed supplement for Roxie. We can only get it from Diss.'

In the shed, Andrew switched on the rafter lamp. The Governess cart sat resplendent to one side. Viewed at that angle the tension of the broad spring was clearly released with no weight in the cart. It was such an effective piece of early balance and poise. Not only did it do the job, it looked good doing it. He thought back to what sales he had attended. Some carts were simply strong and ugly. His had been a find. Its delicate structure relied on that forceful spring which he had worked on for months last year until the shed got too cold. Roxie and the cart would get across that local water splash. The high wheels would easily ride a light flood.

The Saturday chosen for the purchase of the feed was a bright and cold late April day. Bella had a friend for lunch and she was looking forward to a ride that afternoon with her.

'I'll have a bite to eat in Diss. Get Roxie ready and I'll be back about 2pm. That road's open now, by the way. I checked on the travel news.'

'Okay,' Bella called back.

This journey was to be a detour from what Andrew really had to do. He was on his way to Robin, the Farrier and wheelwright at Tostock. He was the chap who knew about the balance problems Andrew was experiencing in the cart.

'You might never set it right, whatever you do,' said this thickset man, as he clapped Andrew on the back. 'Right's different in everyone's head and as for balance - well, that's about as variable as it gets. Everyone has their own idea of the perfect ride. You've restored a poppet of a cart. You'll never get that feel of balance by comparison with a modern car. You can't find the time to use the cart enough.'

After Tostock, Andrew went across country to join the A Road to Norfolk, quite content with those answers and almost ready to deal with thoughts of Roxie. Rounding the first corner of the main road he glimpsed the noonday sunshine on the water ahead. The stories had been correct. The mere was wide water on either side of the road. The brightness forced him a little more awake and in seconds he saw a lorry coming up the hill towards his car, the shining water and the silver ripples on the tarmac. There had been no notices, the road was open and there was minimal flooding across it he judged, so he slowed just a little to allow for water under the wheels. He checked in the mirror for cars behind him. A grey vehicle was just clearing the bend as he had done. And then he was in another greyness.

Andrew's car and the lorry from Diss crossed the water at the same time. The surge of surface water from beneath the lorry lifted Andrew's car off its wheels and across into the parallel mere, lying wind-ruffled on the field. The driver of the grey car slowed to watch a sight he would never see again, a vehicle floating over like a ghost ship from moorings alongside a cargo boat. It immediately began to sink. A roadside ditch hidden by the flood waters was claiming the car before it reached the field. It began to sink rapidly.

The owner of the grey car stopped, got out and began to run. He was showered by spray from the lorry as it passed him floundering towards the sinking car. The man pushed his sopping feet and his wet trouser legs as fast as he could to the vehicle in trouble. He managed to lie down on an invisible kerbside ridge of grass and saw Andrew's hand coming out of an opened window as the car wobbled its way down. He grabbed at it and then he was grabbed from behind. Another motorist had come to help. Together, they got Andrew out of his car and up from the ditch water into the shallower pool on the road.

'Mate! My heaven, mate. I saw it all happen! Let's get you checked out.'

Andrew saw nothing before his eyes but dirty water and had automatically flicked on the windscreen wipers. They didn't start because of the amount of water sloshed on top of the windscreen. Then, all balance left him and he was in a completely unknown motion. He raised himself up from his driving seat, almost as if to get up and out, but to adjust to what was complete insanity. His car was moving over sideways. No braking could change that motion of instability nor its speed. The grey water sluiced away downwards from the windscreen and he saw the empty sky above the line of the hill as a fleeting omen. The car then began to drop beneath him, taking his eyes to his feet as water came in at the pedals and up to his knees before he had time to recover from the surprise. He flicked the window mechanism and it worked. The window wound down and he put his right arm out into the chilled air, intending to move up and off his seat to grip with the left, but as soon as the rising water soaked his underpants and upper legs, he was weighted too much to move up at all. The downward motion of the car and the swift rise of water in it took him out of reason and all thought, except to wave, to let someone know where he was.

The hand which grabbed his wrist was as valued a grip as he had ever known. Then, two arms reached in for his and balanced him before one was disengaged to open the door. Andrew dog-paddled out into shallow water, held up by a man whose arms seemed as long as a punt pole as he guided him. They both flopped belly down in the cold, muddy water on the road.

'My God! Thanks!' said Andrew. 'I thought I'd go with it.'

'Ambulance on its way,' said another motorist wading up to them and Andrew was wrapped in a silvered blanket.

He phoned Bella after a few checks had been made.

'I'll be a bit late, Bella. I'm sorry about that.'

Earning Street

If she hadn't already made her bed, Rosie was certainly going to lie in it. The duvet had been shaken onto the floor. She lay down and spoke to the two cats warming themselves just exactly where she had lain all night.

'Get me a cup of tea, could you, Timsie?'

'Could you ring for it, Tomsie?'

In this writer's head were shredded stories of the old days. Anyone could imagine the lone life - cats, kettles, quite good enough company, but not many take it on really and truly, like Rosie did in Earning Street. No-one knows until they try it, and then there's no blueprint, no list of needs, no blogs. The curtains stay across, the mortgage is long paid off and someone lives on earnings rationed from so very long ago that what had been written and published to pay for it all had gone under wraps, along with the author's name.

'When I'm up, I'll be out all day,' says Rosie to the cats, and you, and possibly they, can imagine the colourless Mac taken from the peg, the canvas bag saying something like 'Farmers Market' and then a shuffle, here, there and everywhere.

Is this really the case? Rose, Rosie, Rosemary, Rosemarie, the flower of Mary, need not do any of these things. She was one to defy camouflage in the upright ordinariness which a lot of people have in Earning Street. Independent means is not an excuse or a privilege, but an element in which some wander with a freedom which looks like imprisonment, and live with a vitality which so easily disguises depression.

The front door clicked on the two cats. They hadn't moved, except to stretch, while Rosie had donned a camel coat, buckled it and gone down to the corner croissant bar, so easy to do in towns with an Earning Street. She had whipped an out-of-date newspaper from her front room grate and her purse was in her pocket. It was so easy to live alone for so long when everything conspires to help it all go smoothly.

Out-of-date news must be quite the thing for a recluse. Nobody knows where you are or knows where your earnings are going. Rosie contributed to an economy of a second-hand past or the past of the second hand. She made sure it ticked away from her as surely as taps drip all night if you hurriedly turn them not quite off.

She had hurried away from it all. The rarely-remembered marriage had collapsed.

'He's sleeping with her. That's enough for me,' was what she had said and meant in spite of her high jinks with Javier, that time in Paris, which could have gone to two weeks and Monty, charming for almost a month in wherever it was in the south of France. Her sense of memory was tenuous even then, when she lived in a London present, ever present as a Londoner, unforgiving as unforgiving London streets.

'They catch the present like nothing else can in my opinion,' she had said to her Publisher on a bright day in October.

'Would you say the same of Paris?'

'Only by the river, Harold. The rest is too planned. The residents don't live it like they do by the smelly Seine. London streets flow like the river. They eddy in backwater.'

'If you've settled here then I'll settle for what you write. It'll sell. You'll get as much as from your New York work.'

Perhaps an author knows all too well that living with your readers is like living with cats. They purr at every comfort coming their way, then they take it or leave it. The rationale comes as a defined flick of the tail tip, found, say, at a cocktail party where only a few raise their glasses and the rest hold them mid-body, non-committal, more top-up required.

The old newspapers said this, whether it was pulling out of Vietnam or the 2008 crash, it was what got itself to the grate-side and then only out to the street café on occasion. Rosie picked one up now. Carefully folded, the Times 1981, January, was opened over her croissant as if to bury it in a dusty tribute to 'Another Strike Warning'. Her hand reached under and along to the plate. Long fingers played with the croissant shape before pulling off a corner to bring it to the light. Golden flakes flew away from her knuckles onto the cafe floor - each for another cat.

Soon it was time to repay her own cats for their morning séance on the bed. They needed to be fed. Rosie stood up very tall to leave. A striking woman of sixty or so in a camel coat, but striking no pose, because the next thing to do was the next thing to do, giving her a degree of engrossment which made questioning an impossibility. This woman always had a way forward.

'See you again soon,' called the Barista with his back to her, but he saw her in the shiny coffee machine, newspaper under arm, the sort of woman who should have had a smart dog on a lead, but who needed no props, not this one.

There had been plenty of them once. Wedding gifts came, oozing expectation, and then bequests in lieu for a town house or equivalent Kensington flat. She kept on board a very great hoard when she had fled, and before Rosie settled on Earning Street, its off-road promenade, sea air, seclusion, a few select residences had dictated their spurious delight to her. Then this street and its prominent name spoke out in the storm of disaster which had driven her from London. Overboard the extras had to go to compensate for loss.

She had inherited several collections of oriental and religious statuettes, of a great age, and more suited to a grand house or small museum. They followed her with their gaze, held her gaze wherever she put them as a quota of the kind of darkness she really could not trust. Just as the Ancient Mariner had been cast off because his eyes swore demonic health, these ancient artefacts would have to be cast adrift. Rosie's cat quota was nil at the time, so the back garden could be used for a bonfire. Tucked away at the back of her home was significant debris for a starter. There were cones from the adjacent garden's silver fir, the October hoard of a long departed gardener, and a few of her books would start a good blaze. For each session, Rosie put two aprons on, one on her back and the other on her front, tying them fiercely in a mirror. She was clad like a gladiator on a cold Grecian day, wary of gods both in front and behind. For their swarthy leather Rosie had undistinguished floral linen, but with pockets for the hammers, the rolling pin and the checklist. Garden tools nearby would do the rest.

So Rosie, strongly built as she was, had stamped on objects as precious to peoples in the past as life itself, to destroy them. Crazedly intent on the blaze, Rosie, cat-less, with no curl of a tail to deter or warn, once begun, took complete destruction as the inevitable conclusion. Everything went of a priceless collection entrusted to her at marriage, right down to human teeth, the almost indestructible. What potent DNA could bring this lot back?

With the books, the treasures, and her writing burned, almost all trace of a former earning life with equity and premiums, was jettisoned. With so much gone, only then had Rosie wanted to read about what she could do for herself, that burnt-out processing plant which rumbled a little bit still inside her, and so she took on the self-help manuals.

Poots she had then, a solid black cat oozing distinction but having none on closer acquaintance.

'I'm up the wall,' was what she said to Poots every morning as her manual went down on the floorboards, her legs up on the wall as vertically as she could manage and she opened her eyes to stare four hours daily at the sixty watt bulb right above her head. It may have gained her at least a few nutrients per day. They were not enough. Time itself tolled.

'It's very serious news, Mrs. Donovan. I'm not sure that we can save your eyes.'

Poots had to go, as did this nervously addictive routine of almost two years, and Rosie sat in darkened rooms wearing shades for over eighteen months, restoring sight so that other cats could come, none of them black.

Then, sight restored, just as in the Bible story, you would expect that book to be her next manual. It was, and its good news, her good news, had to be shared. Anyone who comes from darkness to light has their tale to tell, as if darkness could ever honestly be described or light, around us near permanently, needed any description at all.

She was careful to choose the translation as there were some given extravagant praise in her days as a writer in London, when she was a part of the literary scene.

Rosie debated with the new Poots. White with black paws, Tootsie settled for the name as cats do.

'Got to be the King James version, old girl, hasn't it? You didn't have to sit in the dark as I did.'

Down to Foyles she went on the fast London train, golden camel a touch more faded, and she'd taken to wearing a beret, a fadeless piece of fashionista it seemed, from those pages which never got read of 'The Times' in the grate.

Rosie wouldn't have sat in a corner seat on the train. She was one for the edges. Her long legs needed a stretching space which wouldn't knock others and, in that position, you don't look anyone straight in the face. Coming back, thumbing through a few small, black books, enough to make anyone aloof, she could get on with her life, a commuter with as much purpose as all those returning to the coast at the great cost of a season ticket.

Rosie came at study with the renewed eyes she had been given. She was grateful for the super lightweight, creamy-white of pages which crisply cheated creasing if you were careful. Some may have had a corner turned down inevitably, but even that sort of light crease could be moulded into place by her long fingers and knuckles. She got the Bible pages into shape.

'I'd like these bookmarks,' she said to the owner of a specialist shop of the sort found one per town in this Protestant country.

'That's forty crosses. I'm amazed you found so many different ones, but we order up all the time. We sell a lot of these.'

'I'm glad you do,' murmured Rosie as she paid from the purse in her pocket.

Tootsie, who wheedled an individual way into Rosie's affections, listened to the rustling of pages, shifting of bookmarks, sniffs of contempt and gasps of ideas that this strange mistress let slip onto a warm front room air.

Who knows what Rosie's first time was like? The train to London was a perfectly easy constant, off-peak rate. Use of ticket machine not the Ticket Office, then two buses to Hyde Park Corner, then crossing the road to the grass verge, well-trodden, catching her large feet under the long coat. None of the streets of coastal towns nor Earning Street, have this cachet of chill, exhilaration and exhaustion. Everyone who steps up to speak here finds all three in good supply.

Rosie's pitch was perfect. She had determined never to write again, but read she would, and the one book worth the reading, in this exquisite translation, bookmarked at phrases everybody should know to make their path easier. She had taken a hard path, not the hardest true enough, but it is very hard to hold, the dark. Now she held in her hand that one portion of light which would take the darkness right away.

Stephen looked up at her that first Saturday afternoon. There had been no rain that May. Hyde Park's roadside trees looked in need of a drink, but not him, the saved alcoholic, who had just listened to Rosie's twenty minute opener. He spoke to her as she got her breath after standing down.

'That wasn't too bad, was it?' He spoke blandly. Rhetoric had left the air seconds earlier.

'It's a good thing to do.'

'You'll be back, then?'

'I shall.'

Back she went, about every quarter, taking it all religiously as she did. One Lady Day she stood and half a dozen or so men looked on. She had her rights and how right she looked in the camel coat, the beret, giving her a faded air of a genteel past, or so they may have thought.

It was no such thing. It is no such thing in Earning Street. The sheer dislocation Rosie had courted matched the exactness of her cats. They each gather round comforts when it suits them. Speakers' Corner was a natural draw for all the educated, wild-witted, unknown McCavitys of circumstances none of their choosing. Like Rosie they merely choose to be choosy, not chosen at the last.

Loch Ness

Margaret tapped her four-year-old on the head.

'Daddy'll be back next week to take you to School.'

Aidan looked up at her. He'd been rattling the cereal box, driving his sister mad, so she'd already gone upstairs.

'How long for?' went his next question and three bangs of the box on the table. He knocked it sideways. Tiger uppermost, it lay raising its paws helplessly over a popping bowl of Rice Krispies.

'He doesn't say, this time. He'll take you out after school and at the weekends.'

'I don't want to go with Megan.'

'You did before. Dad took you both up to Inverness. You had a good time together and there were super photos for your Gran.'

'She doesn't want to go with me. She says she can't have Dad on her own.'

'There's never much time for that, Aidan. You both know he has to go off to his work again.'

'Can we go down to London and stay with him?' Aidan began spinning the cereal box around, giving tiger a headache.

'It's only a small flat. Then, he's all over the world in his business and not often in the flat, anyway.'

The weary words were carefully placed. Will had stipulated that neither of his two children should know that he was in Government security and likely to be anywhere on a mission.

'This goes with it,' Will had said when he proposed. It was in a decent Pub in Stirling with just enough background noise for him to speak at a normal volume about the secrets Margaret would need to keep as his wife. Not that the marriage was a secret. It had been a rambling six months or so to settle from rented rooms to a house with a view of Stirling Castle. Margaret's mother in Edinburgh was more than satisfied with that purchase.

'You see eye to eye, then?' Ellen Ramsay was not one to pry, but she set standards. Like many others, she didn't view marriage as a loss-making institution, but neither did she see it as a 'gravy train', rushing onward, building up momentum and savings. Derailment was always a possibility.

Will hadn't been around at the birth of Margaret's first and distress had to be low key.

'Of course, it's unfortunate, Mum, but that's the score. I've got you. Will knows that, and that's got to be enough as things stand.'

Will sent roomfuls of flowers. He was home three months later to find Megan's hair just like his. Facial features develop that little bit later, but there was a good deal of Margaret around the baby's eyes.

At Aidan's birth, his charm was excessive.

'I'm so happy to be here to watch my brave little wife produce a bonny babe. Look who we've got between us. Come on, Megan, meet your baby brother.'

Megan sat on Will's lap at the Hospital bedside, her curly hair twirled by her father's fingers as she reached out to touch her brother's head held close to his mother. This proved to be the family photo for the following year. Margaret made it a trade-mark photo, perhaps more strongly sensing what it represented. Aidan looked unsure of the comforting arms after the womb. Megan was secure on her father's lap.

Will did not like photos taken. 'For reasons of his job', he said. It would be awkward if they turned up anywhere connected with his undercover work. He was rarely in any of the family photos from Aidan's birth onwards.

Margaret reached out to stop the cereal box spinning off the table. She placed it upright to play 'peep-bo' with Aidan as he quite obviously didn't want to go to school with Megan in the car. Awkward ages and stages had to be reached and overcome.

'Now you see me, now you don't,' she said, shifting tiger to and fro. Things had to move on.

'Megan, Megan!' she called in the same breath.

'Mum, I've got Brownies tonight.' She came down the wooden steps leading up off the broad, modern kitchen to their three bedrooms.

Aidan jumped up to swing on the underside of the pine steps as Megan descended.

'This is what he always does, Mum. I ought to tread on his fingers.'

'Aidan, get down. Let's get ready.' Margaret was on de-fuse setting. Will wouldn't want to see too much arguing. 'Calm down for Daddy coming home. He wouldn't have argued like you two do when he was your age.'

'He didn't have a brother like mine, then.' Megan stated with a look in the mirror placed at the twist in the stairs.

'We haven't got an uncle, so we know that.' Sometimes Aidan was just as good as his sister at logic.

If Will had a family bringing him up to land this good job from a University place in Bristol, Margaret had never seen them.

'Your father's family moved to Florida well before he got his job. It's too far for real contact, he says. And then, Granny had died there, anyway.'

'Bodger has just died.'

'Bodger? Who's Bodger?'

'Michael's dog, and he's very sad about it, Miss Cutter says.'

The dead dog and the deadened family came to haunt the few days ahead of Will driving up from London.

Margaret finished up at her Surgery that Friday. It felt odd to be the only one there, as she was a part-time GP. Both Secretaries had been excused to go home early as a matter of urgency. There was a bit of unusual filing to complete, something she remembered from a work placement in Edinburgh years back. The chill metal of the cabinet in the back office irked her. Stashing away cold lives, brought out to be the living flesh when they walked into your room. It wouldn't be long before these files would be obsolete. They were almost all online now and that bit more accessible. Changes were always around the corner.

Will arrived from London closer to the children's bedtimes than she would have liked.

He was wildly delirious at seeing Megan and Aidan again. He handed over London carrier bags containing numerous treasures as if he'd come in on a schooner from Canton.

'Mummy, look at this. When I show Michael he'll forget about Bodger.'

The Scots accents, the new friends, the strange name, didn't unsettle Will. He was at ease straightaway, quite happy to be bombarded. After all, the boot couldn't be on the other foot. No-one could ask, 'What have you been up to?' Margaret didn't, wouldn't, couldn't ask. As they undressed for bed that night, they heard Megan and Aidan chattering on the top landing as if that was all the world there was.

'They really miss you, Will. You can tell.'

'I miss them, too, but I'm busy. I work until the date in the diary says I can come back home, then it's down tools and come.'

If Margaret wondered at all about Will''s work, she compared it with her own. In her job, you held other people's secrets with no sense of exposé, but also without conspiracy. Any consultation involved mutual understanding in the one room. It was that much more strange in the home. It was not the bedroom which resembled the Consultation Room, but their breakfast bar.

'Dad, where's the tie you had last time?'

'Was it a blue one, Aidan?'

'Yes, kind of, but it had a tight knot.'

'Dad won't remember that,' Megan said as she sat kicking her feet against the bar.

'Well, I do, and Mummy will remember.'

Margaret nodded, bringing up the milk jug from the breakfast set they had been given at their wedding. Where did Will purchase his clothes? Were his ties gifts? The sweep of a shopping Mall came over her. Short socks for Aidan, leggings for Megan, a treat for herself on a lonesome trip. She never bought for Will, unless his visits coincided with a birthday.

'I do,' she said. 'It was grey-blue, and you had it on all day, even though we went out to a restaurant.'

Megan jumped down to give her reply. 'Nanjo's, it was. I had a Mexican wrap. I told Siobhan all about it and she got her Mum to take her next day.'

'Well, that worked out all right, didn't it, Megan?'

'Yes, but her Daddy made her eat it all up and she didn't like it.'

Margaret laughed. Will ruffled Megan's hair.

'I wouldn't do that, would I?'

And the reason for that? It had to surface for Margaret as it always did.

'We're not a normal family, are we, Will?' she ventured that evening.

'Nonsense, of course we are. We set standards for our kids, Margaret. I love 'em to pieces. You know I do. Don't think I don't know you do a great job.'

'I'm going full time again when Aidan finishes this first School year.'

'You know best. Megan's getting on well. Girls always steam ahead. She'll have your brains, Margaret.' Will stood up as he spoke, tall, well-suited and close to dapper as an accompaniment to the relaxed manner Margaret had first fallen for. At Medical School there had been plenty of drunks and then the body language of guilt next morning at lectures. Will had been so refreshing when she finally met him in a bar, just like College, but so unlike it as to bring juice to her senses right away. He was the smoothie, too, of course, and she was more than ready for that after so much study. For serious Margaret a serious man with an air of fun seemed to fit the picture.

In two weeks' time there would be half term for Megan and space for them all to be together out of routine. Aidan led the way.

'I want to go up to Loch Ness again, Dad. If I see the monster, I can tell them all at big School.'

'You don't have a chance of doing that, Aidan. You can't see out of the car window like I can. I'll see it first.'

'Well, if you do, Dad can stop the car, can't you?'

Aidan was on Will's lap playing 'long knees' before bedtime. He sat on Will facing forward and he rowed with his elbows vigorously while Will made the lunges forward with him, feet planted firmly, keeping the boat afloat.

'We'll go out in a boat like this to catch him.'

'Can we go then, Dad?'

They knew the hotel in Inverness from the previous year. It was one of a parade of grand, almost forbidding buildings on the road east out of town. It had a menu for children which kept Aidan quiet for almost half an hour.

'I'd like these every day, Mum.'

'I'm glad you're eating up so well.' Margaret's absent-minded reply was brought about by a view of Will's face in a reflecting window. It must have been the pale-grey light reflected off a buttress wall. All the glare of the restaurant lights caught his face as he was eating and speaking to Megan, but a bevelling in the glazing gave him two profiles, attempting to merge as he was animated and then parting company again as he was still. It was a game of light and dark, played with a child, his child, chatting to a father with actions repeated in the mirroring window.

Margaret was due to drive when they set off to the Loch. This was a well-known holiday route. They would stop at Urquhart Castle, its Car Park and the Shop. The dark waters of the Loch would weave their view throughout the car journey, and the finger pointing began.

'Down there in that dark patch, Megan.'

'No, I can see a swirly bit, over here, look,' then over a half mile of so of foliage the chatter ceased and Will looked across at her driving with a smile.

'One day we'll see it, maybe,' he said.

She found herself saying, 'They do it differently now, Will. They search undercover. They send in surveillance, just like you do. Perhaps they even wait for a full moon.'

Will's face changed, she saw from a glance at his jaw. He was looking more firmly ahead, and so, then, did she. She was doing the driving.

At Urquhart Castle the break in the drive suited Megan and Aidan, who wanted to watch the Loch change its colouring. It does that from the high point of the castle and the view must have lured the imaginations of more than the two of them. Margaret's thoughts were tempered with keeping Aidan in tow. Last year he had travelled on Will's back up from the car park, on to the viewing ridge then down to the line of trees which played peep-bo with the view. He didn't need Will this time. He had got over the grumps with Megan and was an explorer in his own right.

Margaret watched the two of them move along the railing together, playing tag, finding the right place for one of them to spot the neck and head and the other to shout, 'I can see it too.'

The fresh air fanned their imaginations. This air could be Loch-cold, at a temperature only Highland Scots know, and this Loch had statistics as well as secrets. It was deep, so very anciently deep.

'Do you think they've had enough?' came Will's voice eventually across a gap of children watching, castle gazing and wide views of the Loch, each of which gave no conversation for them today.

'I'm ready if you are.'

Actually, Margaret was ready, she knew, for a journey without children, one just between her and her thoughts of Will somewhere else. They had journeyed to this known place, readily accessible, easily organised, for distraction, but she felt none of it. Margaret's journey was being made towards a Loch-deep story of Will's life threaded into theirs, dipping in and out like the myth of the monster. It was shown at the Castle. It was history, myth, science and showmanship all together. It was her life with Will as she saw it for the first time.

On the homeward journey, Will drove. She chatted to Megan and Aidan more deliberately than she had ever done with Will around before.

'If you think it's dark down there, it's darker in other places.'

'What sort of places, Mum?'

'Caves, she means,' said Aidan.

'Caves can be explored. You can take a torch and have a look around. Mrs. Pender read us a story once about that. She put some seaweed on a shelf in the class and it smelled awful.'

'Not so much caves, but places you don't know about because you're not told.'

'If you're not told, you can't know, though, Mum. Megan doesn't say much about Sandy, and she's her friend.'

'I don't want you to know, Aidan, that's why,' and Megan almost ended the conversation with an elbow in her brother's ribs. He moved out of the way.

'I tell you about Bodger,' was what he replied from the safe distance.

'Bodger's a dog. Stories are about people and that's more interesting. They have adventures they can tell about. Dogs just go for walks in the park.'

'What if there are stories you're not meant to know?'

'Them's secrets. I don't keep secrets. That's silly.' Aidan was working on his sister. 'They're only for girls.'

'Well, at least girls can keep them.'

'Oh, lots of people keep secrets,' said Margaret.

In Stirling, just as they were negotiating the outskirts, Will spoke to his wife beside him.

'I'll do a barbecue this evening, shall I?'

Open air, an open day. That sounded fine.

Will got Megan and Aidan kneeling up in the kitchen showing his daughter how to chop mushrooms into a barbecue sauce and cutting a string of sausages while Aidan pricked them all over with a fork. The tasks were simple, Will was slick. He was deft and resolute with his children and the two of them loved it. So often food is salvation.

When the half term ended and their usual routine was restored, Margaret had a full day at the Surgery on the Wednesday. Will's month with them was up on the Saturday. He would get in his car and drive away for another three months to an unknown somewhere else. This time for the sake of Megan and Aidan, she needed to know where.

'Are you staying in the UK, Will?'

'I won't know until I get to London. A month is a long time in my business.'

'A month is a very short time for your two children, though, Will. You heard what they said on the way back from Inverness.'

'They said a lot, but you made them say it. Secrets are the unknowns. You said you'd accept that.'

'There are going to be changes ahead, like Aidan's new school. I suppose it's made me unsettled.'

'Too damn right it has, Margaret. I've never known you like this.'

Margaret ended his sentence for him. 'In all our married life. Our eight years of marriage, as you call it, had added up to only eighteen full months with you in this home, apart from when you broke your wrist on that bike ride and you were here a couple of months to get it mended up.'

'Even my work can take account of circumstances.' Will turned as he spoke. A hastily clicked electric kettle began to lightly hum his consternation away.

'I don't think they're work secrets, Will.' She clicked off the kettle beside him. 'I think they're life secrets. I want to know who's doing the cooking and the washing when you're down in London?'

'That's the job. I've told you. It's all in-house and all looked after. It's the way it's done in the Secret Service. You know. You know!' As he raised his voice, he switched on the kettle again.

'You can't drown me out, and you won't, Will. I'm going to spend a lot of time on your secret as soon as you leave this time. I owe it to our lovely kids, and you do, too.'

Will looked aggrieved as he made the coffee, as he always did when these situations arose. Margaret watched him, studying his long, thin fingers, the way he grasped his mug. She had the wind from the Loch in her hair. She would ruffle the waters.

Over the next few months, nothing was easy. Aidan became difficult at the thought of real School and Megan was invited to more parties than was good for her. Strawberries seemed to rule her life all of July until one perfect evening when phone calls and texts held off for more than an hour and she had a breakthrough. The Facebook tracks led somewhere at last. There was a William Logan with an account rarely used in Brentwood and a mere acquaintance appeared to have linked them with one single Like.

'I can't believe it,' she said of her audacity in making the search in the first place. Trust was about to be well and truly washed up and somehow she was ready for the violence of it.

'How could he be in these two places, one after the other?'

The bright screen showed three children pressed together in a family-friendly restaurant, evidently after a pizza meal. They were twin boys aged about eight and a girl of six, not more, between them. In the window, almost obscured by the reflected flash of the camera he was using stood a tall man, her Will.

The man was a definite. She enlarged the photo to study the three children as she might look at her own on a nit-check day.

'They're his. He couldn't take a photo of anyone else's.'

She almost picked up the laptop to bang it down on the table, to dent him as he had dented her.

Then came the clinical decisions. Will became the patient she researched so as to find a cure, not for him, but for her. Her part-time job became just that, just enough to keep her salary, her skills and the trust of colleagues. The rest of the time was given to Megan and Aidan, but divided like her own husband's time, between one family and another. Her solicitor was a respected Family Lawyer in Edinburgh.

'It's bigamy and we'll prove it. He'll get jail for it.'

'When I met with the other wife, it felt right for us both, I told you.'

'Very wise of you to set up a Trust for the children,' said the neatly-suited lawyer from Montague and Soames. He didn't have to answer Aidan.

'Where's Daddy?'

The terraced home

Monica looked at her galley kitchen. It resisted a view, as there was no standing back from it. Its size defeated her efforts to cook and serve up in comfort, even if she could speak to guests across the waist high wall which separated it from the rest of the room.

'I'm going to have the garage taken out of the original build, then that'll be reinforced through to the back, upstairs and down, to give me that lounge diner I've always wanted.'

'So, the galley goes?'

'Yup, it does.' Monica kept that affirmative right through from planning to execution. It became a very long vowel sound.

Any villagey part of London looks very like another. Monica's riverside area had a few parallel streets of artisan housing which paraded itself as choice or chic or charming. No-one mentioned cramped, but day after day for the thirty year commute, Monica knew it. It welcomed her with, 'How did you manage to scratch that suitcase?' from every holiday. The umbrella handle caught the internal door from the porch every rainy day.

Monica tried the road of self-shrinkage.

'If it's shedding a few pounds just to feel comfortable in the box around me, I'll manage.' She spoke to Jade.

'I can't see that dieting's the answer. I should think that's right at the bottom of your list of options to get this place right.'

Jade sat looking towards the galley on a three-seater sofa squashed into a two seater space. 'What's wrong with the place?'

'I want it right. It's never been anywhere near right. It's just convenient for the Tube and you know it.'

'No, I don't, Monica. This is cottage zone. You never made a smarter move than coming here.' Jade was handed a bowl of pasta. 'It's just great for entertaining.'

Monica bobbed out of the galley and knew that Jade couldn't see the person behind the pinny, any more than understand the desire to un-cramp her style of home while getting life lived within its frame. That was the sum of the problem she couldn't tell Jade. It wasn't the home, it was everything in it.

'Come off it, Monica. You can't strip it bare at this stage. You might have thirty years of clobber here and that won't go of its own accord, nor all at once. You'll tear your heart out.'

'That's my aim, Jade, whatever you say. I'm single again now. Got rid of Meredith, didn't I?'

'That was years ago. I remember it. It was the M&Ms, I called you then.' Jade's pensive look was not intended to remind her friend of the break, only of the bright things.

Monica's outlook changed from that moment. It was not the reminder, but that she had been reminded so glibly, as if a new window on the past was coloured in by Jade, or any friend who thought to embroider her life with skeins and threads she no longer possessed. She would take her time, but be thorough with the changes, moving as if with a steady waltz because she'd been asked to dance.

The dance began. Monica stood in the centre of her living room and tried very hard to cram all her possessions in it. Offload the visitors' bedroom first, with the cream lace curtains, the duvet pale mink to blend, cushions, a book or two, the dressing table. Meredith had found the stool for it. Camden Market had been a stomping ground of his before his hair became just that shade of grey when stallholders begin to doubt your earning power. She'd forgotten that the stool was underneath it over the years, pushed out of the way, gathering guests' belongings when they came.

'Damn, damn, damn! Under the bed, I've got boxes and boxes from that event I did with the local dramatics. Pippa and James never did come for that delivery when they said they would.' Meredith hadn't even bothered to chase them up. These heavy boxes should lie on his chest until he coughed them up and out of her bedroom. Thoughts of storage costs came crowding as Monica held her mug, not in her dream of a ballroom for the dance, but on concretely cold warehouse flooring, all so that builders could put the extra room in her terraced house.

Her house hadn't been there in mid-Victorian London. It was a modern infill of a previous archway and alley for horse and cart. She'd seen the photos of the street at the local Library in grainy black and white. A while before she had come to buy, a flat roofed garage had been built right through to the back of the narrow terraced house for one car space, a utility room and cloakroom. It was one long wall from front door to the French doors onto the garden.

'And as naff a piece of planning as any nincompoop could do,' so Monica realised only after the first few weeks of occupancy. She didn't want out at that stage, but she didn't want that wall. Now, under the approved planning application, width was granted.

'It'll feel like a palace.' Jessica and Neil had called at the Bank Holiday weekend.

Only half recalling the dance floor which had turned sour and become the warehouse floor, Monica moved into the fine entrance hall of a palace as soon as the couple had gone. Columns held up her swell ideas.

'There'll be acres of space for the widest of smiles as I open the palace door,' spoke her elevated thoughts to her small lobby. Then the bottom step of the stairs caught her shrinking gaze. There were almost half a dozen objects balanced on top of a shoebox she had recently filled with CDs, classical, for someone.

'I can't believe it,' she called to herself and clapped her hands to her head. She sneered at her hands now. Guilty, they had paid for stuff and accepted it at a till. She placed them on her hips, willing her whole frame to heave the entire upstairs into the road to make an immediate outdoor market for neighbours to scramble and buy.

Her Market stalls would stretch right down the road from right to left from her home. She'd have rugs down at the river end, nicknacks and electricals centre and soft furnishings up at the town end to entice. She'd unpick the whole house. It would be done solo. She'd wear a bandana.

Over that week, that month, that near-draining close-on-a-year, the moving of effects went on. Almost everything in the original long, narrow, build needed to be sorted, packed, labelled and put in her own and neighbours' cars for a journey to storage, and still she had to sleep and feed. Just herself, of course. She wasn't thinking of refugees, but she'd know one if she met one in a dream, perhaps. On the television, watched when she was crammed into her bedroom, they always filmed large families of strapping lads, wide-eyed little girls and mothers with their own mothers. Where was the solo female, the one misfit brutalised by loneliness, and the crush of far too many objects attempting to fill any vacant space?

'That particular blouse is a row with Meredith,' she said under her breath to Jade one day. An astonishing number of carrier bags were lodged in the lobby and Jade had to peep. She was expected to do so.

'Is that really the reason for it being flame red? You're kidding.'

'Wish I was. It was one heck of a row. I'm finding that even a paper clip speaks a thousand words about how I harboured that man.'

'You make him sound like a criminal, Monica, and I'd thought it was all so sugary. M&Ms, remember?' Jade's face couldn't keep up the pretence any more. 'Funny how we don't say these things at the time.'

'Yeah. I use paperclips all the time, but they don't use me.' Monica's face couldn't be seen because she had bent down to tuck clothing into one of the bags.

The shape of every box irked her. Was there a rogue in every room, even the attic? Monica had thought her parents' things were up there, but no, one suitcase set her off on a voyage of extreme distaste. She stepped back down the loft ladder, padded down the longer flight to the kitchen and stood in it to deliberately make a cup of English Breakfast tea. She found a cup, not a mug and then a small teapot at the back of a top cupboard.

'He was turned on by those damn olives, I know he was.' She had smelled the air of Skiathos as she pushed the suitcase to one side. Glass platters placed on glass tables and the blue of the pool swirled together in her mind's eye, as if they were buoyancy aids for children chatting in opal seas. She spat at her tea.

'I don't think cups do it for me any more.'

The entire home was to be bulldozed by her determination before the architect and his men removed even the garage door. The upstairs was to be held up on several girders over the course of the building work and numerous floorboards had to come up, as did the carpets. That moment, that momentum in rolling up a carpet, brings the dream of perfection, an empty room. Making it happen was more like a nightmare.

'Lift it over, Jade, can't you?' Monica couldn't see her from behind the wardrobe.

'It's got to twist first, Monica. Right, no, sorry, left.'

The bulky object was levered out on the top landing. Getting Jade back in the room looked impossible and yet the room was empty. Even so, space congratulated her and straightened the curve of her struggling back. The carpet cursed her. Now Monica could see the indentations of the divan feet, mincing impressions of those Meredith moments remembered from first to last. She was glad to see Jade squeeze into the room to roll up the pale blue, faded remnant of any cloud nine.

There were a few weeks to go before the bulldozers came. The demon of destruction had not quite taken hold of her enough, she felt, and this is where her sister, Mary, came in.

'Family'll help out with the big stuff, Monica, as you're on your own over this.'

'I don't want to be confessing and apologising for furniture I should have removed years ago. It's there, so it's there!' Monica's unreasonableness was all part of the course. Managing Mary had been a lifetime's study.

'We'll get it all moved on Saturday. Des has got the day, the van and a man. You couldn't ask for more.'

'I know, Mary, I know.' Monica knew it was easier to deal with objects than deal with her sister on a mission.

When the very large items had gone, the house took on an air of resignation matching Monica's own. Third bedroom had a word for it almost, spitting at her, 'Happy to be happy about it!' It was as if every room was a stage set for a season of Plays. Monica could breeze through and choose her minimal scenery in each one.

The bathroom, however, remained implacable. It was a medley of styles, rather as toothbrushes are. The fixed bath mocked her with its overdue longevity there in that cruel space of relaxation. The airing cupboard held such an array of horrors that Monica shied away from it.

'The damn things were invented to make a muddle,' she said pensively to Jade.

'What have you got in there?'

'Oh, you know. There's even flannelette sheets from when I was a Girl Guide. I can remember Mum chucking one in with the sleeping bag come Camp time.'

This hug of warmth from the airing cupboard was stultifying. Scents of school swimming pools, toes curled at the end of the high diving board, Meredith's armpits, meandered round her cheeks and chin. She enlisted Jane in a hurry.

'Get it all out, Jade. I'll pop down for the laundry basket.'

The garden trug had to serve and was carried up to the first floor. The linen, laundry and towelling looked as dishevelled as a man before a shower.

From the toiletries cupboard, Monica jettisoned almost everything on the trug. It looked a mess because it was. Monica detested the thought of its years in the closed cupboard, losing its scent, gathering dust to its sticky caps, presenting a battalion of battered beauties, odourless and shapeless.

'That's that, then?' was all Jade felt she could say. There is no comment to be had for other people's toiletries.

One day before the crews were to arrive, when Monica was almost ready to move in with a neighbour for the duration of the work on her terraced home, a knock came on the door. It crossed Monica's mind that this would be a final caller on the old house, before it assumed its wider frontage and more pleasing approach.

'My God! Meredith!'

On the concrete doorstep was a man so obviously near sixty years of age, you could half make out a medal on his lapel saying so. Grey hair was scurfed up from small ears over a large, squared head and below the open shirt jacket, his buttons were haphazardly in the wrong buttonholes, so that one shoulder looked higher than the other.

The 'Oh' of surprise forming on his rounded lips came out as, 'Monica, what have you done?'

'What do you mean, 'What have I done?' I'm having the house re-fitted. What's it got to do with you?'

'A hell of a lot,' came a lamenting voice from the lips still shaped in retaliation. 'I've been changed into a dervish, Monica. I've been going round in circles, searching for things I know I never had, like a bad dream on the go.'

Monica grasped the realisation as if she had had been handed a bouquet of flowers. Her acceptance speech could have been rehearsed.

'I realised very early on that I was doing all this for you.' She moved to close the door. 'I'm very glad that you were able to get involved from the wings.'

Benjamin's Cup

'You'd hardly know it, Ben.'

'But I would, Essie. That's the point. I'd know.'

The husband and wife were discussing Goss ware. Ben had detected a slight crack on one handle of a two handled cup, crested very brightly with the arms of Scarborough.

'I've never chosen to collect junk and I'm not starting now.'

Ben had been a collector for twenty years, ever since University days. Grandparents, originally from Latvia, had arrived in England with nothing. This was a way to pay off student debts. He stood with Essie now at one of many cabinets filled with the finicky perfections of the dedicated collector.

'I'll put it to one side. I'll get something for it at the next Car Boot sale. They won't know there that Goss miniatures have to be the real deal.'

'That's three Saturdays away. I've got to get Laura to Ballet.'

'Oh, yes, we'd agreed I'd get Kevin to his football game.'

They nodded to each other at their dedication to the family ideal. This was what they had planned when they had adopted first Kevin at six months and then Laura at nine months twelve years ago.

'He mustn't miss that and I've got to come on from Chertsey. It'll work, if the weather's on our side that day.'

'It'll work.' Ben pocketed the small cracked pot after wrapping it in a piece of tissue paper. 'I'll leave this for the next Sale and I mean to get to that one.'

Essie remembered that Scarborough cup. The first crack had appeared in the family, too. Ben got back from Chertsey, but Kevin wasn't to be seen. He wasn't ready for the game and he had no intention of playing for the team.

'What do you think you're doing? You're letting them all down. Some of their subs are rubbish and you know it.'

'I'm just fed up, Dad. I'm fed up with being picked up and collected. I don't want to play ball, that's all.'

And so it went on, the pull in a quite different direction. Kevin pulled out of everything. It couldn't be argued that he was worried by exams. Instead, he very easily persuaded Laura to join him in skipping almost everything there was to skip, including bedtime. It got to be every night the same, that the two adopted children were always somewhere else.

'Laura said she'd be back from Lily's house, but you just never know. Her phone's off, of course.'

'Kevin's sorted out at Pete's, apparently, but we can't know for sure.'

The worry was interminable and recriminations as keenly fought as a deal on a sale at a Fair and with an equally untrustworthy outcome.

There were some might never came back on the deal, just like Kevin and Laura.

'Do we believe in collecting? No, not me and Laura. I'd like to take a hammer to Dad's head for the number of times I've been dragged to a sale and he'd be nose down in a fusty old cupboard telling me he had a find. I'd bang it, crisp and sharp like an auctioneer's hammer at the end of a sale.'

Kevin's clipped phrases startled his friend.

'I knew you couldn't get on with your Dad, but kids often get it wrong.'

'I'm not one of them. He bragged us into the complete humiliation of owning us, as much as the junk on the shelves.'

'You don't own kids, Kevin. They're just yours.'

'Well, they'd paid for us, see, and now we're paying them back. I've been gone a couple of years now. I've been in London. Laura went to Bristol. Now that's a place.'

Sam shifted up closer to Kevin. 'So they say. I haven't tried it yet.'

'It's your next trip, then.'

In Bristol, Laura was an uncompromising house guest. She lived with a friend's parents.

'Do you know,' she said, 'they'd worked out how we could help them on the hunt. We were used like sniffer dogs in barns where the house clearances landed up. We'd get rewards, too. The chance of our favourite pizza before we drove home, provided we'd washed our hands.'

'How long had your Dad been collecting before you came along? Some people do make it an obsession, like anything else. I could be obsessed with housework, but I'm not.'

'Yes, but even if you were, it's not like collecting. Our house got so full, we'd have to tiptoe about.'

'I don't collect. I'm more likely to be de-cluttering, not the other way round.'

'Just what plays into the hands of collectors. Dad'd take a look at everything. I felt I was digging in a tomb, and used like a tool.'

'I'm sure they didn't mean it, your Mum and Dad. How long since you've seen them?'

'I gave up going round a few years ago. We both left at sixteen to get away from it. All the good intentions they had, and they blew them.'

Laura looked up from the sofa where she had sprawled from an all too brief overnight sleep after her Bar job. 'It was like we were shop bought and had to be carefully looked after to remain looking new. But we weren't new, we grew.'

'Everyone's entitled to grow up.'

'Well, we grew out of their image for us. We didn't sit still to be dusted or polished any more and that isn't a crime, is it?'

'No.'

Laura phoned her parents one day in July.

'I've got to be over your way, so I'll call by.'

'You what, Laura?' Ben was taken aback at the abruptness.

'Aren't you pleased, then?'

'Of course I am, but your Mum's not been too well.'

'I can't help that, can I?'

'But don't not come, Laura. When shall I say you'll arrive?'

'I don't want fuss, Dad. I'm just coming, right.'

Laura walked up from the station at Frinton-on-Sea. Almost everyone did. The town deterred the casual parker. She didn't have enough money to look in the shops along the High Street and probably only the newsagent knew her now. That was the trouble, the older parents. Children stood out in a retirement home of a town like this.

The family bungalow was reached by their own alleyway, she had always thought. Just a tidy strip of concrete, but it led somewhere for her and Kevin each time they set off on an errand. They talked like conspirators. Every child does this, imagining they are the only pair to do so. It eliminates the need for anything else, a very satisfying situation. Laura once knew where every dandelion was likely to grow.

Ben opened the door with a flourish.

'Hi, Dad. So how's Mum, then?'

'Laura, I'm fine,' said Essie, coming into the lounge. 'It's only high blood pressure. I can cope. Sit down, I'll get you a coffee.'

'Thanks.'

'This is very unexpected. What have you been doing with yourself?' Ben took the mug his wife gave him. 'You could have kept in touch.'

Laura looked up at her mother, took the mug and put it straight down on the coffee table.

'I'm out of trouble now. I've left the Unit and now I'm on a study course.'

'Well, you'd be good at that, Laura. You were always so bright. Kevin found it harder to keep up.'

'Don't keep criticising, Mum. It's all you used to be good at.'

'Laura, stop that,' Ben stated calmly. 'Your Mum can't take that any more. We've moved on.'

'Oh, I suppose I haven't? I have you know. I'm finally out of the rut you put me in.'

'I said stop that kind of back chat, Laura. Get to the point. The past is the past.'

Laura picked up her mug and said what she had come to say.

'I can't get on without a decent laptop. I can't afford one and I thought you could help me out.'

'Oh, Laura,' said Essie, 'we've given you so much. What have you done with it all?'

'Mum, it goes, like money always does. Me and Kevin didn't grow up the saving kind.'

'We're not going over that ground again, Laura. How much will you need?' Ben looked at Essie to be compliant.

'A thousand. It's a lot, but I'll be able to shoot ahead.'

'How long do I get to think about it?'

'Stuff that, Dad. Sell some of your precious collection and make it happen. I can't believe you've both still living with it all around you.'

'Don't talk like that, Laura. That's not exactly negotiation, is it?'

'No, but it's either buy or sell with you. I'd never make a buyer of your sort of stuff.'

'Maybe not, Laura,' Essie came back quickly, 'you need up-to-date stuff, we know that. Will a thousand cover all the start-up costs? Can we hear how you are getting on if we agree?'

Laura drained her mug.

'I've got to get started first. I'll get as far as I can. It's not everyone gets on the course I've got.'

'We'll transfer it to your account at the end of this week. Is that soon enough?'

'Yes, thanks Dad, it is.'

Laura's return wasn't as fanciful as her outward journey to Frinton. She was on her mobile to Kevin for some of the way.

'Mum isn't too well. She's lost a bit of spark. The house looked just the same, up to the ears with china and glass, as always.'

'Don't even think to tell me. I'm not over the moon remembering that. What made you go so suddenly?'

'I needed some money, Kevin, like you did last year when baby Tom came along. I didn't go begging. I put my case and they agreed.'

'Oh, did they? Dad must be easy to push these days.'

'I told you. I made my case. I'll be going again, but not too soon. I want the first couple of terms to go right.'

'Well, good luck then. I may drop Mum a line, but if I think about it too much, I probably won't. It might bring on a heart attack.'

As he pocketed his mobile, thoughts of Tom took over. Taz had taken him over to Frinton when he had got cash from Dad last year. He hadn't seen his son since then. 'He's mine,' Taz had said and had gone.

It didn't take too long. Those three letter words, 'Dad', 'Tom', 'Mum', had an effect. Quite what was going on, he couldn't say, but he found his way to an Antique Shop in Twickenham High Road, not an attention-seeking place. Its facade had worn with the main road and not very well, either. Kevin looked resignedly into the window to begin with, then went in.

No bell jangled as he had half expected. A gentleman close to retirement age looked up from a desk at the side of his long room.

'Looking around?'

'Yes, I will.'

At Kevin's first glance, junk appeared to fill the shelves. Over and over again he thought he saw the same sort of plate, saucer, teapot, jumbled at angles on shelves so full, one awkward brush by would have consequences. He realised that it was what the browser would want, a sense of muddle so that they could make a find. One level of establishment up and it would be a different style altogether. It would be tidy, demonstrating nothing but the shop owner's expertise.

Kevin had heard all the queries before. He went over a few from the past when he would be rummaging with Dad, turning round and then hear Dad saying, 'I'll have this. I think it might be worth a fiver, I'll give you £3.50,' and that was that.

Then he saw exactly what he would haggle for. It was a piece of that crested china Dad and Mum had once collected specially from the rest.

'I don't suppose this is in perfect nick, is it?' he asked the man at the desk.

'I don't even know if it's the real thing, mate. I'm only sitting in for today. The owner doesn't get much of that stuff now and then it isn't the real deal. You'd know, wouldn't you, from the style?'

Kevin couldn't pretend to be a collector, so he just had to say, 'I'm thinking of my Dad. He's got quite a few. They look like a collection of mushrooms, they're so white and clean and round. It's for the colours of the crests to stand out.'

'I was told that all the best ones are in museums. It's very unlikely that this is anything but a copy.'

'I'll have it anyway. I've got to make a stab at something.'

'You can have it for £2.50.'

In tissue paper, this lightweight miniature cup, sporting the arms of nowhere more exotic than Morecambe Bay, lay in his pocket on the way to the Underground. There must have been thousands made for that popular resort, but it didn't matter. It was wrapped, so it was a gift.

'Kevin! It's Kevin, Essie!'

He hadn't rung ahead. How did he expect to be received? When it came to the opening of the gift, Dad didn't flinch at all.

'Nice little item, Essie. Look what Kevin's brought us.'

Cherry

I really like being called Cherry. I would watch Mummy saying, 'Let Cherry do it the way she wants,' to Daddy over breakfast, when he was up-ending the milk over my cereal. If I had poured out the cereal, why shouldn't I pour on the milk?

I have found out since then what very different things they are, cereal and milk, put to use every morning as a partnership, when they are not, really.

'Put your hand here,' Mummy would say and I did. I raised my right hand over the cereal bowl to feel the pop and spit of dry goods wetting.

'Teasing the appetite with sight, sound, smell and taste for fullest satisfaction', was what it said on the back of the packet. You would be able to take on the day ahead. Mine was without sound.

I read and read. I moved on from cereal promotions to Fairy Tales then Cambridge, which seemed to me to be equivalent jumps apart. All I had to do was to sit and watch the teller of the tale and then the lecturers, who used a sound system of no help whatever to me.

Then the divorce went through and I was off to University to bond with Mummy as best I could in Freshers' Week.

'We'll get a flat bought for you,' she slowly mouthed. I could deal with all the paperwork, soundless stuff online anyway. She told me, 'Daddy will never know.'

It's a good thing, sometimes, that no-one knows what you are doing. There are so many things I can't know because no-one has looked my way to tell me. I smile up my comprehension, but I don't know anything at all except a manner of interpretation learned at the breakfast table over milk and cereal. When to pour has become important.

Then there was a new baby, I looked at Mummy and saw many words for the first time.

'This is your half-sister. We will go to see Daddy and his new wife to congratulate them.' Mummy closed her lips then, like she does when she has lip balm in the winter. 'The baby girl isn't deaf.'

It was good. Whichever way the second Mrs. Fielding and my baby half-sister turned, we would be there. It was when the time came that half-sister had quite grown and questions were being asked, that we moved on and they did not know where.

I wasn't to know how our new neighbours in the north would take to me. Everything's such a gamble when you lip read. When the couple took against me and told Mummy that I was stand-offish, I was the fish in the bowl with my mouth open as they circled round. Living next door and disputing a line of land right outside the kitchen window, their strange behaviour could be seen as 'freedom to exercise', but it didn't seem to matter about mine.

She said it was to get away from those neighbours that Mummy took me back over to Daddy and the growing teenager, over and over again. We could circle there, much as our neighbours crossed and re-crossed our kitchen window in their own manic way, when I'd be caught washing up or stirring a sauce. I couldn't hear them coming.

What a training we had in covert surveillance, for the Court case we were forced to bring against them in the end as much as anything.

'We have to write everything down, Cherry. How else can we prove what we know?'

Canker or not, we moved in on the prey. We drove south sometimes as much as three times a week, telling Daddy it was to fit it in with hearings in York or Manchester. The city life and its parking seemed to suit us.

I sat in the car a great deal, whatever colour or make it was year by year, and remained watching until I was needed. We joined in the celebrations, too. The half-sister's Graduation set us back a bit on finery and so did her Wedding only a few years later. Each time Mummy got ready as if a major feud might erupt.

'They will want us both smiling,' I often said when Mummy's lip-balm moments came on, summer or winter.

'Of course they will, dear. And we shall.'

I wondered if Mummy ever dreamt of life without me. From the time it became clear that it was she who would always have to make everything clear to me, she must have mused about her independence and mine. I began to tot up any gains and there weren't that many really. Mummy had aged and so had I. There were always legal delays. There were always consuming winter days.

The disputed boundary was a miracle wreathed in snow.

'It isn't there any more,' Mummy would say on the really wintry days. If only concerns could disappear under that cooling plaster.

'The Ice Age has retreated,' I'd joke to Mummy, when it all left us on a warming wind.

I live all the time in a world where sound is taken away by a blanket of snow. Outside our farmhouse on the moors, the entire landscape is shaped by silence. I could read the books and articles which told me so.

Then one summer day Mummy told me, 'Daddy isn't at all well, Cherry. You can see the text yourself,' and she put the mobile phone on our kitchen table. It read 'Tests show advanced Cancer,' and it was a capital C right there. Daddy's diagnosis had my initial. That would end our trips, our watching and waiting. If there was going to be grief, it would be almost thirty years too late, or like the text, 'too advanced'.

'I'll organise some final drives.'

Another spring came. The moors were lovely. Daddy couldn't walk them, or cycle some newly opened routes he would have loved. I sat in the back of the car with him on the way to Scarborough, speaking carefully about the views, not Mummy's views on his condition.

'It would never have got this far if I'd been with him,' Mummy's mouth line was tense and remained an open O. I patted her arm.

I couldn't be sure how the years made that much difference. I was born for dispute and Mummy and Daddy argued as much today as when she had left him.

'I'm not taking that turning to Scarborough. It's the long way round. You know it is.'

Daddy's lips said, 'Tell your mother, I'm happy either way.'

It was not so easy on the canal. A two day trip was booked for a dying man. Mummy seemed to want Daddy trapped at the last and was convinced that this would be a dream of his fulfilled.

'Some like a hot air balloon flight,' she had said at Daddy's first trip in another element.

It felt like being underground. Daddy lay, wheelchair close, Mummy fussing and really good with omelettes. I had the holiday medicines for him, although Mummy was the guardian angel, authoritative about doses and steering the course she had plotted.

And the end came. Daddy died in the arms of his wife at home and not in a Hospice as was recommended, and there had been a rift about that too.

Further north, October winds began to blow. I watched them take the leaves whilst on my every shopping trip to Whitby at the end of that year. Mummy dropped an invitation for Christmas.

'Cherry, I have thought of a way back.'

'We haven't been invited back,' I had to reply. 'The funeral was three months ago.'

'You won't mind driving will you? The forecast isn't too rough.'

I don't hear windscreen wipers, nor music in the car. Mummy sat beside me, peering, like me, at the changing view of what we knew so well, the route to Daddy's house.

'There'll be discussion of the Will. It still might all go to Probate and Rhianna is on her own in all this.'

The Peaks sat squat alongside us as we drove that day. They were constants. Mummy could not keep still.

'Are we going to the house? What have you arranged?' I said. 'Have you heard from Rhianna? How is she coping?'

I couldn't get a reply in the car and Mummy didn't attempt one, but she tapped in the post code of a service station on the Satnav.

'I know the house, Mummy.'

She stuck the note with its post codes on the dashboard. It read 'Needham Social Club'.

'That's where Daddy had the Writers Group wasn't it?'

'He did,' Mummy must have said as I detected a firm nod out of the corner of my eye.

The satnav spoke on. I watched its map in front of me and Mummy nodded me through my route. Roads of terraced housing, the staple of the Peak towns, smartened up and quite well-lighted in this early December evening, deserved a cruising by.

We pulled in at a clear piece of kerb and stayed in the car a good half hour. A few men came by, probably going to the Pub I had seen on the corner.

'Here's one.' Mummy nudged me to look at her.

A tall gentleman in a mackintosh and carrying an umbrella came across the front of our car. I could see the intent look on his face and one hand holding a folder under his arm. He looked a lot like one of the sort Daddy had said attended monthly as he had done for a good many years. I didn't know about the writing they did, but this man had been effusive at the funeral. They had 'lost a valued member'. They were 'privileged to have had him with them', I knew he had said.

In this dark, I nudged Mummy in return.

'I am joining the Group,' I saw her say in the half light.

'It's such a long way to come though, Mummy. They don't know you at all. Maybe they're all men.'

'We're here now, Cherry. I'm going over.'

Mummy got out of the car and crossed the road to a stone-arched double doorway, incised over with the name of the Club. I wondered if the men would be kind to Mummy. It wouldn't be a drop-in Writing Club. You had to join this sort of thing and pay.

I caught up with her as she began to go up the concrete stairs just ahead of a well-lighted entrance hall. There was a notice on the door at the top, and Mummy opened it on six or eight men and women handing round cups of tea.

The tall man definitely said, 'Welcome', and Mummy had a chat to him.

She turned to me to say, 'I'm staying for the evening. What about you?'

'I'll sit over here.'

Years of questions came across that table as I watched the lips of as many as I could. Sometimes I only caught replies. It was the replies which gave me the questions I wanted. Pieces of paper were pushed around occasionally. The man in the mackintosh spoke to Mummy most often.

'He attended regularly. I can't give you examples of his writing. We just take those home with us.'

Mummy spoke to them as if she was leading the group. The politeness of each gentleman was making for a very stuffy room. They listened as closely as I watched.

'Do you think it wise to continue when Rhianna Fielding has joined the Group as a tribute to her husband? She'll be here next session, she told us.'

'An extra member, Rhianna or not, shouldn't exclude me or my daughter, should it?'

'I think I'm only going to say that it remains to be seen.'

That was it. Mummy got up to go and so, of course, did I.

The journey back in the light with a light-hearted Mummy beside me, was broken by a trip to York.

And then a ghastly winter set in. It was clear from the charts that a journey down in January might be problematic. The Probate was due for settlement and Mummy made this an excuse.

'You can't use the Writing Group for a squabble.'

'How else can I get to Rhianna on neutral ground?'

'They'll turn you out, Mummy. You're not even local.'

'They can't turn me out.'

If it was a journey, it passed. There were so many outrageous moments I didn't let on to Mummy. I relied on that coffee after our evening meal that day.

There were two distinctive women among the men in the room at the top of the stairs. One was a speaker and the other Rhianna, who was sitting with arms folded. She was expecting a fight and she got it from Mummy.

'I'm entitled to be here, like anybody else in a free country. I want to be where my soulmate expressed himself,' Mummy said.

Rhianna's face reddened. The two bereaved wives were looking across wide boundaries.

The booked speaker left the room to find an arbiter, but places like this don't employ Caretakers any more. She came back to Mummy's shouting and mackintosh man's reply.

'We have to get on. Unless you go as our Committee has agreed, we can call the Police and hand it over to them.'

I caught almost all of it from near the doorway.

Mummy came over to me. The room shrank her.

'Daddy isn't here. It's only friends who knew him,' I said.

Court appearances

'Emilia is saying exactly what you told her to say.'

It was said with the tautness Jerome carried with him as a constant. Like the military precision of their wedding in Madrid almost ten years ago, she saw a stretch in his shoulders, as if epaulettes were balanced there to keep him parallel to the Parade ground below.

Below him now sat a clutch of Jury men, come not 'to dine', but to feast on the cross examination of his wife. Catriona, clear-sighted Catriona, was in the witness box and, only metres away from the rail she was clutching, stood her husband telling everyone what it was she had not seen, only imagined.

She was clutching at many things: straws of sorts, bundles of papers, the waists of her three little girls. She clutched the bannister outside the bedroom door where she had first realised foul play was playing a part in their family game. She gripped the rail so hard that she had bright red palms when she finally caught up Emilia in a tight hug.

'Daddy couldn't have, Emilia.'

A line of Jerry's antecedents crowded the upstairs landing as she spoke these words. Military men. Men with sons stepping firmly in a father's shoes, men of the world, a fighting world. They each clapped to attention.

It was Claudia. She came out of her bedroom clapping her hands.

'Found my teddy, found my teddy bear!'

Another one to hug, protectively, as she had never done before. Loving, giving, every hug, but not this one today, by the bannisters, keeping them from harm, in their own home.

Jerome had been working late that night and wasn't due back until ten, she had firmly at the back of her mind. Catriona's clear mind, the University educated, powered-into-shape mind, which she wanted for her girls, too, Emilia, eight, Claudia, six, Davina, four, a near perfectly balanced trio.

Jerry stood out in the Court area.

'And she does exactly what you tell her to do.'

Slimly dressed, matador-styled almost. Attack was his defence and he stood with pride in a manhood he knew he possessed and was going to keep. It was time to reply.

'I have made nothing up. Emilia told me that you had been in her room to read her a bedtime story as you usually do when you have an evening to spare, but she told me something else was also happening. It was always when I was out.'

It was that hug, caging them both, looking over the bars along the landing to listen for Jerry, the father of them, and none of the births had been easy. She winced at her anaemia, the infusions, being attached to wires and tubes and the help she couldn't give herself. Catriona, needing others' blood for her own offspring. Jerry had been in every time. He had been looking for clues.

'Mothers love sons.'

This hadn't been the first of these conversations. They'd been the silent subject matter on every flight to Spain to see Jerome's mother and brothers in Madrid. Presenting one family to another was on his mind, as if an Infanta needed to be pleased then clap her hands at the pretty image in front of her and cry, 'More, more!' Catriona's girls were such careful, hard, hard work and so beautiful on arrival that they dispelled the ugliness of pain at a stroke, but there was still Jerome. Three girls, and then the Obstetrician's warning that there should be no more children. Just thirty and a child-bearing wreck.

'Can Emilia pin-point this on a calendar? Does she keep a diary? Of course she doesn't. You fitted that remark into place for her. You've spun a fantasy into a truth and you can't do that. It's all lies from start to finish.'

'Emilia told me what I'm telling you. Of course, Claudia and Davina didn't hear what she said and, if they had, they wouldn't have understood. They're too young.'

Her husband's head moved to gaze at her from waist to hairline, undoing her blouse with his eyes, leering sophisticatedly enough, except she hoped he'd fumble on the top button. He did not.

'Of course they are, all three of them, too young. Emilia knows what a loving cuddle is as you snuggle up to a good book, that's all. And that's all there ever was.'

'I have to disagree strongly, Jerome. Emilia didn't make the actions she described sound very comfortable, never mind loving. You were casually brutalising her.'

Dressing gown cords, pyjama trousers, Daddy's trousers, were all in the mix of Emilia's descriptions, once Mummy had her on her own, and was tempting her with hot chocolate. Catriona wished she could have switched on just a lone spot from the kitchen ceiling. Even dimmed, they all gave out a bright, early morning light. Catriona longed for a candle. It flickers in penetrating darkness. And she had to probe. How much had gone on? How much had Jerome made of all the moments with his daughters?

A candle flickered its aloneness in her. At one remark beginning, 'Daddy came into my room when you'd gone out that evening,' Jerome had isolated his wife from all real help. Fear ignores any practised personal armour built up from the dealt body-blows in a school playground, for instance. It denies armour its place in all history. It can do better than that. It takes the fight to the centre of pride, hollowed, useless, and collapse is inevitable.

'Daddy didn't hurt, but he might,' Emilia summed up her bedtime story experience matter-of-factly.

Jerome appeared to take a step forward. In fact, it was his shoulders thrusting, then relaxing as he replied.

'Those are very strong words. Emilia is our firstborn. I've known her the longest. I know her well. She loves being out and about with me. When you had Claudia, then Davina, I was the home carer whilst you recovered. I've got a very good relationship with Emilia. She would not make accusations against me unless you prompted her.'

'My mother came over from Norwich to do most of the caring.'

In the bluntness of her remark came relief. Keep sentences short. All else is self-serving. Children foremost, self last, and the argument will be won.

It was dispute from the first grip of the bannisters, where she had stood in sheer fright, calming one daughter after the other, producing a domino effect as bedroom doors opened and the girls jumped out and into her arms. But a disputant is more than a mother hen, clucking and fractious, she had to gather the facts and they were in very short supply.

She knew she had stayed on that precipice of fear for far too long. The girls' remarks from that all important moment should have been recorded. A play script was what was needed, tapped on the iPad with detail determined, but what would have been the use? Now words about words were needed for Family Liaison. Their bland faces were just over her shoulder in the courtroom.

'My job doesn't allow me a lot of time. When they were young, I did my bit.'

'It isn't the beginning which is under discussion. It's what's been happening since.'

Jerome and his girls. Catriona was looking at his looking at them over the years, as they were handed into their people carrier, strapped in, helped out again, jumping into their father's arms and calling, always calling, 'Daddy!'

'Mrs. Fonseca. Our panel will want to know the effect of the accusations on your family life. We'll begin with your husband.'

What might be released? Catriona knew that tensing of the spring ready in Jerome the moment she broached the subject.

'What? What are you saying? I'm not an abuser. Where has this come from? It's from all your deliberate misunderstandings and there's been quite a few.'

'It isn't about us, Jerome. It's about them.'

'No, Catriona, you've put a children's army into position at your back. You needed back up!'

'It's not I who am using the children, it's you. I believe Emilia. What I can't believe is how you've betrayed our trust in you. We should all be safe in this home and, unless you can explain yourself, we can't be any longer.'

'I'm not explaining away an accusation as fanciful as this. They're my girls. They're my girls.'

Weeks, then months of this denial. Jerome glowed each evening as he arrived home, readied to heat up the quiet ferment Catriona hoped would balance out each day. It boiled over regularly so that Catriona took refuge upstairs where it would be quiet. Daddy didn't trespass on the dark any more, but he drove the girls to school. He still had to be in the action. He was planning a move closer to the Campus where he lectured.

'Dr. Fonseca, thank you. I'm sure we all find that very clear.'

Catriona's hopes swung on nothing at all but her life ahead with the three growing girls. Davina, dark-haired and dark-eyed like Jerome and robust, taking all the changes in her stride. Not so with Emilia and Claudia, thrown together into a life where Daddy only peered in. Madrid Granny came to stay for a week and took them out to the cinema. She wore red clothes with scarves which kept her head afloat in Spanish silks. She spoke so nicely to her grandchildren and angrily to Catriona out of earshot.

If wearing red wasn't enough, Jerome seeing red was another thing all together.

'Your mother, damn her. I won't have her near,' and 'Tell your father to pickle himself, the retired rustic!'

Only school holidays saw Catriona and the children over in Norwich, and a Christmas there was, piled high with presents.

'That's clear to us all, too, Mrs Fonseca. Thank you.'

Stood down, they were, at long last from the Family Tribunal. The months of waiting for the hearing had covered the mild days of a late Spring, bundling its seasonal pastels around the home where Catriona had things more in hand.

'I'm planning to take the girls out to Sunday lunch in two weeks' time. Have them ready, Catriona.'

'That isn't reasonable, Jerry, and you know it. It worries Emilia and she doesn't get off to sleep. Why don't you call by and cook them up something in the kitchen? They'd be much happier.'

'That doesn't go for me, though, does it? I'll come at twelve thirty.'

How she wanted that finishing line, the judgement. It was a hard-fought race. She had the mother's baggage, the caring which bears down and makes the going hard. He had the lighter load, burdening her now with the phone calls and away days, tossing concerns which didn't concern him, towards her, like plaiting her long brown hair, as he did with his fingers when he lay in bed beside her so many disagreements ago, with grey.

The letter of resolution came. The decision of the Family Panel was 'Near-equal access. For at least two weekends in six, the three girls must stay with their father.'

Sherbet Lemons

If Bryan's face muscles jerked, he wasn't aware of it. He had smiled, as he almost always did, at the absurdity of the committee including him and expecting a customary input.

'I'm not built for that,' he had said on a double abseil one day, 'I'm built for this, open air breathing.'

Jock and he were alongside on a popular local crag. At the base, the University Climbing Club members stood to watch, kit on the ground beside them, hooded faces raised to the two leaders in admiration at the clever timings of the two men and the rugged outdoor ballet to which they each aspired. Synchronising, stepping, hanging accomplished, these two men were walkers, sure-footed and sure of their territory.

Bryan ran Orienteering, Jock the Climbing Skills. The distinction was clear and separate lectures given. Bryan issued plans and routes. Jock kept to safety basics from base to top and back to base. Only cold air drew them together.

At his allocated flat in the Freshers' wing, Bryan was part of a unit set up to deal with student problems, working closely with the Student Union body. Cilla was liaison, Pete the muscle. They had to meet.

'I'll be all right for Monday about nine. Lectures are at ten.'

'Where?'

'That side room off the hall.'

The three arrived at the same time outside a painted black door. It opened to reveal a small office, bin empty under a lightweight table, four or five chairs around a window with closed, narrow Venetian blinds.

'This is it.' Bryan's shoulders sagged as he sat down. Cilla took a chair opposite and Pete sat beside her.

'Quite a few emails have come to me about lack of directed study.'

'That's an old chestnut. It means they're wondering why they ever came to Uni at all.'

'I've got another five or six about Tuition fees.'

'That's dealt with by the Bursar's Office.'

'Accommodation looms large. Seems that the smart places are damp and the downbeat ones are expensive.'

The conversation between Cilla and Pete continued persuasively, with Bryan forward in his chair listening and nodding. He said nothing.

Nothing rang hard on the clear, clean floor. It jumped up at Cilla in so sprightly a shape that she inadvertently spoke her mind to it.

'We all ought to speak up.'

Pete stopped his onward flow.

'Each of us has an opinion,' he said, and looked at Bryan.

In that shapeless box of a room the three looked out of place. Large-boned Bryan didn't fit the chair, Cilla's slight form silhouetted the curve of hers and Pete had yanked one hip and both legs towards the door.

'If we could have an agreement on the date for the Climbers' Dinner, then I've got a positive statement for each and every one before I rabbit on in the email about putting up and shutting up.'

'You can't make things that simple, surely?'

'I make sure it all sounds personal, if that's what you mean. I write individually where I can. That gets to room-sharers, too.'

She looked pointedly at Bryan as she spoke with an ice-pick of a challenge.

'What's your point of view?'

Bryan moved back in his seat in reply. No sigh came from him, no sound came from the chair where he had shifted. Instead, there was a rustle of crumpled paper from one hand in his jacket pocket, and out came a bag of brightly coloured sweets already opened. With a slight, but careful movement, Bryan tipped the sweets out across the empty table between them. They were sherbet lemons, yellow, crystalline, even through their cellophane wrapping, clashing on the table with a shout of discomfort and tipping haphazardly to halt all conversation. They sat disconcertingly childish between the three adults. Bryan bent down to lob the empty bag into the bin.

'Fine,' said Pete.

Cilla felt compelled to do more than glance at the puzzle in front of her and its manoeuvring. She was drawn to the shape of the wrapped sweets, the uneven butterfly wings on each and the overlapping so many had taken up as they came down in the throw. Here was query. Each sweet ready to be eaten, each space between them wordless, and the discomfiting visionary who had thrown these around was unwilling to speak.

'I'm off to sort it, then. Time's up.'

Pete left with her.

'What was all that about?' he said at the turn of the stair.

'I don't know, and I'm not so sure I care. He'll email us that date. I want to get on.'

She didn't feel as confident as she sounded. Everyone needed Bryan's expertise. What kind of awkward customer was he to keep counsel when it wasn't required?

'He tipped out the bag and left us looking at the sweets,' she said to her flatmate, Reeta, 'and I'd like to know why he tried making a fool of us. We were only doing our bit for the Club and the students. It might have been boring but that's normal.'

"He who laughs last',' she quoted in return.

'We can't get back at him, if that's what you mean. He's done the job a few years now.' 'Perhaps that's what it's about?'

'More than likely.'

The date for the November weekend climb had been set and the Friday evening before travel in the minibus the following morning was Group time, a heady essential of introduction or re-introduction to the climbers who had expressed an interest at the Freshers' Fair. Some had stayed the course or lapsed from last year. Others wanted a taste of freedom after a lengthy stint of study. The Union foyer filled up with bags and equipment. There was all the commotion of a Friday night coming on and Bryan slipped in. He had crossed one of the busiest roads in the city to be at the door. He had mounted the dozen steps outside to be available, and there were no carrier bags in his hands.

Cilla knew all this because she had watched him come in. It was her slot on Reception desk, so it wasn't easy to keep an eye, but across the bending of backs and students sat on their backpacks, crowding but passive, Cilla could see the man with the pocket full of sweets, dressed in a mid-grey kit of the best label in the Outdoor trade. She saw him go upstairs where the Function Room had been booked for their evening rendezvous.

During the next hour, Cilla assumed that Bryan would be keeping his side of the bargain, to produce a meal for the twelve of them. The students would bring the beers.

That hour later, Cilla went up to see how things were going.

The room was large and square. Its add-on was a galley kitchen which was very easy to use for cook-in events of this kind. Two long tables had been placed at right angles near the kitchen corner and the blue stacking chairs ranged along and behind. The table was laid. Cilla came up to the corner to look more closely. Each table setting was meticulous. Cutlery, napkins, glasses, table mats to match, gave off a considerate glow, but as she approached, Cilla knew from an undoubted silence that something was wrong. There was no one working in the kitchen. Bryan wasn't to be seen.

She stood over the table, willing it to be a statement of intent, endeavouring to smell chilli con carne from the kitchen, looking at each fork as if to reach out for its trembling as only just being put down in a hurry, but no, this table was a static and meant to be so. It froze conviviality as if entertainment was the last thing in the mind of the host. In fact, it was. No meal was intended to be served. This 'Mary Celeste' of a table was meant to haunt her. It did.

'I tell you, Reeta, when he came in and caught me staring at it, I almost dived for cover.'

'That same guy with the sherbet lemons?'

'Yes, Bryan. He leads the expedition groups. He'd laid it all up and deliberately left off the food, like anyone with an empty stomach would be held there as a kind of torture.'

'Oh, come on, Cilla!'

'No, I'm right. Then we got to hear a bit later, when everyone started to arrive, that he'd ordered in pizzas. What d'you think of that? We sat like dummies around an empty set up, right, only to have boxes dumped on it, all wrong!'

'Bonkers,' said Reeta.

Next day, in mid-Derbyshire, the minibus was parked and a small group had set off to climb. Cilla joined in the commotion. Pete was there, after all, seeming taller with the gear he was carrying. It was that ever-resilient colour, muted orange.

The deep-set lay-by served them well. Cilla stood to look over fencing and dry stone walling towards the mid-morning easy climb. Bryan and Jack had gone ahead, pacing Pete and three others through roughening fields which rose to the indeterminate scree climbers love. It has a sound under boots all of its own, Cilla knew. It was anticipatory scrape of rock and, on return, it securely congratulated the climber. Above the short cliff face sat a patch of deep blue sky in the surrounding grey clouds. It would shrink or widen as the day allowed and was as much a part of the close haul of climbing as the surface grit and clammy rock. It was destination.

The figures became smaller and were quite enough reduced for her to set off and find them halfway through their climb. The others wound with her on the walk to the centre of the buzz which was their lives. Climbing leaves you emptied of all but your own resources, concentration countermands fear, and trust in a group which buys into the whole thing is an imperative.

At their arrival, the advance party was well on its way up. Pete was on the left with a partner, Jock and Bryan had taken centre and round on the right the other pair had committed to a twist of a route. It looked interesting. They'd have a lot to say about it when they came down. Cilla was going to be looking up for about a half hour or so she reckoned.

Wade spoke beside her.

'He won't say much.'

'Who won't?'

'You know who. Bryan.'

'It's Jock who gives us the debrief, usually.'

'Yes, and don't we know why.'

It was Wade, determined. Cilla could see him gazing up at that clear blue emptiness she had noticed earlier.

'He's the sort who's best pleased with this silence. It speaks to him. I heard it whispered he'd been turned down as a Catholic Priest. That's rich! We all have to take part in the emptiness of his life.'

FAS7 MUM

Sophie sat behind the wheel, relaxed. She had said, 'I don't especially want it, Martin,' but he'd insisted. To really make it hers was an entirely different thing, just a matter of time behind that wheel. Her new numberplate was meant to be seen on the very fast roads themselves. Roving would confer the frisson required. How soon could she get up the speed to speed off?

'Martin says you've done it,' spoke son number two. 'I'm off to study, job done! Now, it's time for yourself.' He'd gone a month ago to the same red brick as his brother.

If it was reward for her hand in getting them that far, it felt a bit flat, she had to admit. If only she could lift up the new number plates like the outsize cheques raised by winners of marathons or a lottery. She sat, book-ended by an envied and expensive promotional statement she couldn't see. She was concertinaed, making the music, driving the action forward. Where would she go? Bristol for the M4 run 4 Mum. She was thinking in number-plate speak since Martin had presented her with this image of herself.

It was a mild November day and a bright one as she looked up from the dashboard. It would be one of those days with its eye on chill winter, daring it to approach quickly, and yet the sun would be down at its soonest for the time of year, bringing street lights and headlight dazzle for longer than you would really like.

She made up her mind to head for Salisbury by cutting across country from just beyond Peterborough. There'd be enough fast lanes for her new commitment. A1M, A45 at Northampton, a deep down curve of a drive, then M40 for the great stuff over the Ridgeway to meet the lowering sun glinting on MUM. Enough flourish in that route plan, enough roundabouts to pause and power forward and at the end of the journey, the hotel and the Christmas Craft Market to convince her of a purpose and season for all things. The approach of an appointed season is concerning, we have Scrooge to remind us, even if earlier than he would have thought possible.

Sophie wondered if sleek suited her or just the car. Martin's seven year old Audi had been hers for a couple of years. It was red, the sort of red that pleaded for high polish else it looked like a variety of plum from a B&Q tin and several coats of it at that. The Olympic-style circles made her giggle a bit. They sat above her number plates like suitably raised eyebrows or open mouths or even as perfectly polished and rounded top teeth smiling kindly at the less speedy and every other rogue on the open road.

Into her journey now, Sophie was above Milton Keynes on an A Road she knew well. Stony Stratford was not far off and the road was like a switchback. Thomas had clutched her hand once, Freddie had crouched forward with Martin. Whose shoes was she in, aged forty-five and still perched for speed with an anxiety for each of the foursome, reading the dial on their bodies, hair raised at the back of the neck, hers straying forward over her face even in a wind determined to blow it behind? Both hands came off her steering wheel to quickly sweep it back this November. It was past coffee time and she'd take the break at Newbury. She'd pull off the road at a Coaching Inn, and very appropriate for her thoughts, too.

She was a bit stiff as she bent for her town shoes. Low, dapper heels, navy suede, squarish toe. Then, car boot opened, long, cavernous, and taller than she could reach, the red lid allowed her as much space as those old London stagecoaches. All wood and leather, they had lettered on them the posts of gentility, the County towns. In between was wild. Fast roads flattened the serious worries of the age. That travelling public travelled seriously and, like them, she was here to take a breather, best foot forward, rolling in on their ground floor. She took up a menu card, just in case she lingered longer.

The boot closed sensibly enough when she returned only a little replenished with walnut and goat's cheese salad. FAS7 MUM lost its shadow and glanced up at her with an uncommon daring and familiarity.

It was time for faster, if the A338 would allow it. There'd be dapper villages to slow her, children at gates, crossings for schools and shops with push chairs, all in the wink of an eye. The once she'd left Thomas outside the shop for a loaf of bread in Oundle, she would never forget. Her knees shook for a few seconds as she drove on. There was plenty of dualling after all. Even the dashboard grinned with relief at the steady speed and the clock asked the question, 'Why the Christmas Fair?'

She had always been a last-minute dash mother at this dashing time of year. Like many others, she'd made attempts to be careful, judicious, cautious, canny even, at Christmas, but each year the manic speed of others drew her on. Unlike elections, Christmas is close to one hundred percent turnout. This year, Sophie was going for fast track, early buy, beat the crowds, craft items, Cathedral town Fair, a whizz.

Crossing close to Salisbury Plain, the road slipped by Danebury Hill. White Horses were near. She knew how the Plain took the driver above the downland mist into the intrepid emptiness found there, as undecorated and undisclosed as an out-of-town factory complex might be at the long Christmas holiday break. There, bleakness extended itself right and left, and pecked grass blades looked just as they were, minutely attacked by loneliness.

Then, it was Old Sarum on the right, spire ahead and the Hotel a comforting corner, riverside, wide parking. Number plate nosed in, neglectful of its rear, to face a high brick wall. Sophie swung into action in her snub-toed shoes with all the eagerness of the newly-arrived and was quickly known by numbers, her debit card, her number plate. A great log fire glowed as it should, two sofas beside, and she parked herself there for a coffee with Baileys. So treat-full a time of year and there were two days ahead without driving. She would be early at the Fair tomorrow and sat to imagine its being set up, the tensions of occupying space which humans hate, space where others are. She had enjoyed the drive down and now she would drive herself on through what crowds came early to these well-advertised events.

Next morning, the lightweight lift brought her to the ruby carpet of the lounge measured exactly up to the silver door. It was so easy to slip through from a sense of movement to sobering civilities with strangers.

'Are you here for the Fair?'

'Fairs are very tempting, I tell my husband.'

'Have you been to any abroad?'

The careful shoppers were there all right, in her hotel. They'd managed a long drive as she had. They had car boots ready to receive the goods. They had lists an arm long. They bought for others, too. It was part Calais booze-cruise, part Cathedral Close niceties, and the sense of swelling pride at making herself a part of this suffused Sophie. She was even patted on the back by one Phyllis, grapefruit and two boiled eggs with toast, as she was finishing a breakfast coffee and ready to go. No return to her room. Sophie was fully primed.

Like a pretty village in a town, each stall was substantial, roofed, decorated and designed to please on sight and with what few shoppers had come from their hotels this early, Sophie could still see between legs and arms that there were last minute deliveries. Santa's hats on heads disappeared from view to delve into sturdy boxes. She saw a hand from somewhere underground place a steaming paper coffee cup on a stall. It was going to wobble. Sophie reached out to straighten it for the unknown groveller, who surfaced just then.

'Oh, didn't see you coming. You're early. That's best. Where are you from?'

'I'm East Midlands.'

'Where are you staying?'

The coffee was lifted up, grasped by fingerless knitted gloves, and there was time to talk.

Numerous details of the planning came tumbling out. The cold air grasped the breaths of the two women as they exchanged roles, one emphasising the need to be there, the other the need to come as a supreme right whichever way round it was. That need to be busy, useful, and then to relate it all over again. Tilly was her name, stall holder for five years, at once levelled with her first customer. She sat on a stool to chat, eyeing the other stalls occasionally. Things were quite slow at this time of day.

'They're ideal places for forward planning. Good for you.'

Away from the number plate, only slowed by the cram of stalls, Sophie made her way from Tilly's pitch to the far side of it all by noon. She took her time over lunch at a café on the longest road in the town where they were more than ready for crowds. She watched from a window, delighted at the build-up of trade. Her phone calls home were full of praise as to how it was being handled.

'You didn't have to tackle Christmas so early, Sophie, but that's you.'

'I'm perfectly okay, Martin. I really am.'

Tomorrow, the Cathedral, she told him. After hotel lunch, which she'd booked at the earliest time, she'd set off.

'Back before dark. Make sure of it, Sophie.'

'I shall.'

Returning the keys, the Receptionist smiled at her as she deleted the car details from the iPad.

'So you'll get a move on then?'

'I'm sure I will.'

It was the right-angled approach to return. M3, London's Heathrow outback, then M25, that most uncertain of roads, to link her to the A1 all the way home.

She was fortified, declared her number plate, quite as humorous at top speed as caught in a slowed queue. She'd never had to consider her back so much. The rear, the posterior, most noticed, least talked about, for all the inner remarks of the well-resourced man, 'Nice one!'

Every gear change around London brought her up against it. She'd look in the rear mirror far more than she ought, but easily, easy about the action. Martin had said, 'Go steady with things,' and that was what he meant. Your rear is your own affair.

When her car was finally facing north, she took more notice of the sky. A benign light might be hers for the two hours, covering ground fast, lights on at Sandy, perhaps, powering up the London clay road, Bedford's brick fields a little distant, Peterborough's remaindered quarries much closer to the road. She was tiring now, true, inside a box which comfortingly moved, but not for much longer. She thought of the gifts to gird herself for the final push home. Once, she had mightily feared that she only bought for men and choices were limiting, teasing her into wardrobing the three of them at the stroke of a Christmas brush. She had overcome that. Her gifts were edible, home-grown, handmade. Ladles lifted by human hands and persons who timed their mix, produced the outcomes. She liked that, and they would, too. They would appreciate this final, personal touch.

The drive crackled under the wheels as she pulled slowly round to half face out, boot beside the house door, only a coir mat away from the hall's warmth of home.

'Steady!' called Martin loudly as he came out of the house to greet her.

The quiet whirr of her cleverly-adapted car boot determined the end of the journey. A well-greased metal arm came forward from the opening, jerked efficiently round and deposited her lightly-built mobility scooter on the gravel beside her door. Her swivel seat took her as close as a slick jerk would to get her rear on it with no more than a sigh, she and the seat each.

'You've done it, Sophie. I'll get the bags. The door's open wide. Get yourself inside.'

Multiple Sclerosis had brought Sophie to this final Christmas. Her early gift, the number plate, had really given her plans a lift.

Washed up

Shropshire borders a wealth of byways. A jiggle of lanes promise yet more miles into the far reaching hills and off those enticing routes lie farmland and rolling woodlands prized by the gentry of two centuries ago. They employed footmen in their Halls until the Fifties. Mothballs would have been the salvation of a mustard serge waistcoat, and breeches could be shortened if need be.

Jilly's husband remembered his parents' footman when he was a boy at Monwell Hall. He wasn't wistful or resentful. They were the emotions he had to put to one side in order to operate in a régime which had itself resolved into another kind of tasteful decline. His wife now kept the whole place going at her pace, which was phenomenal. Two sons had moved out years before. Wystan and Jilly ran the Hall alone. Along with a woodman, the Park was her responsibility, too. Jilly organised Bluebell Walks, Snowdrop Tours and Daffodil Teas for Charity and was patroness of numerous local good causes. She was of the all-or-nothing brigade from their formative years in the War. Even now that Wystan could do only the minimum to help out, Jilly rarely said no to requests.

She had said an emphatic 'yes' to eight guests arriving in mid-October and for a quite special reason. She could easily cook for the ten in total. She'd planned meals for forty when there was plenty of help, but the couple leased into the attic flat had aged and could not be usefully employed any more, so her lone tasks took careful planning.

'I'll make fish pie, Wystan. You like that don't you? After all, it's a Friday they are coming. On Saturday we shall be off your back because we'll lunch out in Shrewsbury.'

'I've got three bottles of a good white. Will that be enough?'

'They'll bring a bottle each, I expect, so we'll recoup.'

'Get some fruit for dessert, Jilly dear. Don't overtire yourself.'

'Oh, rot, Wystan. I'm going to do frangipane tartlets. They're easy. You can whip the cream.'

The House party still represented the raison of their fine red brick house so admired for the trim colouring of its day, when locally quarried stone was considered impossibly vernacular. Each symmetrically positioned sash window looked onto land, that explicit gentry ideal, each chimney smoked across a dewed valley creating its own shapely fog when fires were first lighted. The double doors which footmen once opened still faced up to the sunny south and, if closed more often in these current decades, commanded the portal between inner and outer splendour just as firmly.

Jilly employed her precision thinking in a less than precise kitchen area. Its drawbacks were the first things remarked upon by the guests between themselves.

'I can't believe Jilly's offered all this to us,' said the Butler.

'Especially when her kitchen is so small,' said the Cook.

'There's all the beds to air,' spoke up the Housekeeper.

'They evidently need to keep up appearances,' replied Lord Osward.

'Time for a photograph?' Jilly came into her Drawing Room with Wystan. 'My husband, Wystan, everyone. He knows exactly who you are from the filming. Gather round this sofa.'

Wystan stood to take the photographs required of this unique reunion. The group of friends, thrown together as colleagues, had worked for almost a month one year ago on a TV series set in a large country house during an invented Wartime Shropshire. Just as they had done for the filming production photo, ladies sat. Lionel, Lord Osward, for whom Jilly had acted his Lady, stood behind her, then Gamekeeper, Chauffeur, Butler and Gardener joined him. On the sofa with Jilly, three energetic ladies who had auditioned as Cook, Housekeeper and Teacher of the evacuees, smiled broadly. Hilary, the Teacher, had arranged their reunion. They were each of them here and it was time for smiles.

'Unbelievable, that it happened.' Jilly was first to get up to look at Wystan's attempts.

'Jilly's been so good to have us all here.' Hilary spoke to Wystan as she rose. He needed a seat himself.

178

He sat down on another sofa to observe this group whom he had come to know by their antics in the TV series. They were the House party and it would quite probably be one of Jilly's last except for family occasions. He looked at his animated wife, the hostess, the figure who had been the linch pin. In the filming the evacuees had acted up to her goodwill in housing them.

'Did you enjoy the series?' Hilary sat down beside Wystan as everyone chatted on.

'I did. I could hardly believe Jilly fitted the part of Lady Osward so well. We never did have a title. There was just the land when the Gillands arrived here. You can't have seen it yet, arriving this late. Take a good look tomorrow. It's glorious at this time of year.'

'She was our natural Lady. The children wanted to get their manners right for her.'

'She's always a stickler. I think she's ready to show you the house, now.'

Jilly had attached herself to Gardener, Colin by name.

'Wystan's mother owned it. It was handed to us in 1948. We plan to hand it on to our eldest son.'

Jilly's tour was precise and informative. It was friendly and naive too, in its way, Hilary realised. This woman, who had been picked to act as a Lady in a remote Shropshire House in wartime, chose to promote her own time-warp of a home as someone prepared to go on to the bitter end. Jilly placed its very fragility as a strength. She coped, and this house they each felt they were viewing through Jilly's eyes alone.

'This magnate began it all,' said Jilly in front of a floor to ceiling oil painting of a gentleman in breeches. He was stood looking over a gate to a woodland walk.

'John Gilland made his money around Manchester and Liverpool. Quite a few like him came down through Cheshire to buy land and show that they had made it.'

Later, she was to wave them towards unused rooms along poorly-lighted corridors, then to open the doors of their allocated rooms which had been aired. The windows were slightly opened to a mild October and a hot water bottle was placed in each double bed.

'I'll come up to switch on the electric fires when you're at sherry.'

Jilly came into the Drawing Room from the house tour with all eight of them. Here was the roaring fireside, and how supremely it worked in the well-proportioned room.

'Sherry now, Wystan.'

Jilly left her guests to talk and went along to the preparation of the meal, then upstairs to close windows and turn on all those electric fires.

Of course there was a chorus of 'Can we help at all?' expected and politely refused. Cook had already brought her homemade pâté and toasts for the starter to the kitchen on her arrival an hour ago. Butler had agreed to bring a cheese board with grapes. The two had been delighted to contribute in that overflowing sense of camaraderie which being thrown together under camera and lights had brought to them that year ago.

There was one trolley wheeled in to begin.

Hilary looked round from her position by the fire and saw Jilly's bent figure beside the trolley which held the heavy china serving dishes. What an array of equipment for a meal, prepared in what was so small a kitchen. She touched Cook's arm and moved with her towards their hostess.

'Jilly said that years ago dishes would have been brought from the kitchens with the ranges, right down that long passage. She showed us the nearer kitchen, but it was so cluttered, didn't you think? She and Wystan use it for the two of them as it's in their wing. She's done all this from there.'

'Must have. What a star.' Cook's praise was well-directed.

They moved off at Wystan's request into the dining room while Butler manoevred trolley one. Jilly came in with vegetables from the hob, each well covered, trundling trolley two up to the table.

'Please take your places. We'll enjoy your starter, Cook.'

These were passed to each guest and finally Jilly sat down.

'Wystan, we haven't done this since last Christmas. We welcome the opportunity everyone, so do begin.'

Hilary saw them all forsake their roles immediately. The conviviality of this setting took away the strangeness they had originally felt in revealing themselves on television in the starched roles of a faraway time. Here was now, and as house guests they could be themselves. None of the courses lost heat from earthenware dishes. The fish pie was hailed as a masterpiece, belts were eased just enough and old Gilland and others might have beamed down at these ten, brought together only because he had made the money in the first place. But it was Hilary who had emailed and persuaded each one of them over a period of six months to mark this occasion at Monwell Hall. The meal, which stretched into a lengthy evening, was an achievement for them all.

Hilary remarked to Cook. 'We'll offer to wash up. What do you think? There's masses to do what with the glasses.'

'It's the least we can do.'

Butler was talking about his family of two young boys and a wife who had walked off. Lord had confessed earlier to a dogs's life in North Wales, never having married. He lived the nearest of them all to this remote spot. Gardener had a penthouse in London's Dockland and didn't seem to be green-fingered in the least. New light had been shed on each character gathered round a table in candlelight with enough said to satisfy the level of curiosity dinner parties demand.

Jilly's pride surfaced as soon as help with the washing up was proffered.

'No, I won't hear of it. I'll manage very well in the morning. Let me show you up to your rooms. You've all come so far.'

Short of placing the empty plates on the two trolleys in adequate piles, there was nothing for it but to get to their respective bedrooms. There was no TV room, although Jilly and Wystan had a set in their small wing.

Wystan led everyone to the Billiard Room.

'This was after dinner recreation, then?' Chauffeur remarked and Wystan nodded.

'Not so very long ago.'

Hilary and Housekeeper had been given adjacent rooms. Cook was led down a further corridor where there were bathrooms for each guest.

'Goodnight and sleep well. We'll aim for breakfast at 8.30am shall we?'

Hilary opened her bedroom door, gave a brief wave and retired.

As the door shut behind her, she understood Jilly in an instant. This proud lady with a robust past did every task in the house herself. Hilary gazed around at a perfectly shaped and designed bedroom of the Fifties. What few modern items were in the room; the clock on the mantelpiece, the new electric kettle and the china jug of fresh milk so carefully placed beside it, were outclassed by the faded, genteel modernity of a different age. Photographs of the family stood on every cupboard and chest of drawers. No ornament or vase escaped a lace mat beneath them. Draped across small tables, neat runners caught at the dust which had doubtless hastily left the room only the day before. It spoke of use and collective memory all at the same time.

It wasn't a room to forget, and then there were all the others she had been shown on the tour, colour-coded and each with a flower name. Hilary had a bedroom of spring crocus yellow. Only one more move was required before she slept, to set the alarm for 4.30am.

In jeans and a sweater, this hour of the following morning saw Hilary taking a torch down the dark back stairs. Closing the kitchen door, she turned on the light and pulled the curtains across as the blaze speared the front lawn. As soon as it was light she would open them again and catch up with the dawn. Then she turned to take stock, and it took a little while. She imagined herself in a bivouac in the Crimea or Mess tent in Sebastopol. She was on duty and duty had to be done in this mud-brown and ochre-coloured, well-used kitchen from round about the era of her bedroom's golden chintz. Its over-use rather than its lack of cleanliness struck her. How could a Christmas dinner for a dozen be cooked in these confines? Hardly more than one person could wash up.

'Right,' kept leaving her throat, softly, as if telling the goddess of routine herself that she was in charge. No goddess of anything faced these piles as Hilary did, feeling Jilly's worn and aged hands in her own as she worked. The hot water came through without a splutter and the electric kettle to top it up didn't make too much noise as it boiled. She got cutlery in to soak while she washed the glasses.

As she picked over the trolleys, piled equal sizes of plates, clucked over the state of the stove and shortage of table space, the gods came to her aid. Hilary found a small stack of trays between a cupboard and a wall. She levered them out to be her clean surfaces and found a small stool on which they could balance before the trolleys were wiped down. She could not know where everything went. That would have to be left for Jilly.

Hilary almost expected Reveille to be called as she checked the curtains at intervals to discover dawn. When it came, on this strange October weekend in a little-known backwater of an inland county, no soldier peering through a tent's flap could have been as prepared as Hilary felt for a new day. Ahead of this house were the hills, black, rearing up for a piercing sunrise to distribute its bounty on their lower slopes towards her. As she gazed, leaning her elbows on the draining board with large tureens upturned there, Wystan's land, the far trees, then the sculpted garden became grey, then pink and then gold, if green catches at gold as Hilary thought it did at that moment. She turned off the kitchen light minutes before and the window slowly gave the County's sunrise to an early riser, and a good deed done. If its complexion was just that little bit rosy, Jilly of all people, needn't be the least bit embarrassed, nor held to this task for what would have been half the morning. Every item had been washed up.

Lightning Source UK Ltd.
Milton Keynes UK
UKOW05f2338280417
300165UK00001B/123/P